¡JUVENTUD!
GROWING UP ON THE BORDER

Stories and poems edited by
**René Saldaña, Jr. and
Erika Garza-Johnson**

¡JUVENTUD!
Growing up on the Border

Stories and poems edited by
René Saldaña, Jr. and Erika Garza-Johnson

DONNA, TX

Text copyright © 2013 VAO Publishing.
Cover image and interior photos copyright © 2013 Ileana García-Spitz.

ISBN 10: 0615778259
ISBN 13: 978-0615778259

VAO Publishing
A division of Valley Artistic Outreach
4717 N FM 493
Donna, TX 78537
www.vaopublishing.com

First printed edition: March 2013

TABLE OF CONTENTS

Poetry

Author Biographies

Acknowledgements

"God's Plan for Wolfie and X-Ray" originally appeared in *Twelve Shots: Outstanding Short Stories about Guns,* edited by Harry Mazer. Bantam Doubleday Dell Books for Young Readers, 1997.

"The Heartbeat of the Soul of the World" originally appeared in *Face Relations: Eleven Stories about Seeing beyond Color,* edited by Marilyn Singer. Simon & Schuster Books for Young Readers, 2004.

"Combustible Sinners" originally appeared in *Combustible Sinners and Other Stories.* VAO Publishing, 2012.

"The Noise Expert" originally appeared in *High Plains Literary Review,* was also performed in "Arts and Letters Live," Texas Bound Series, Dallas Museum of Art, and was published in *Appearances,* Lamar University Press, 2012.

Dedication

René—*Para mis padres*, René and Ovidia Saldaña,
who showed me a love of reading by themselves reading a lot
and out in the open, the *Bible* and *Selecciones*, respectively.

Erika—To my father, Jesús C. Garza, who taught me how to love
my family, myself and this great place we live in, the Rio Grande
Valley, who taught me how to be a poet. To my mother, Delia P.
Garza, who taught me what it means to be a strong woman and to
fight for my dreams. To my brother and sister for teaching me the
importance of a good education by example: thank you for your
guidance. To all my teachers who saw a spark in me. To my best
friend Lady Mariposa, who helped me get over my shyness when it
came to reading my work in front of a crowd. Most of all, to Rob
Johnson, who made certain everyone would know that I, too, was a
poet and that I would be a mother to two wonderful children,
Cactus and Isabel.

Preface

HINDSIGHT, THE SAYING GOES, IS 20/20. IN OTHER WORDS, from my current vantage I can look back on what's transpired and grasp its significance when then I was clueless on the matter. This newly-acquired insight is usually made the better because in the time that's passed I've also picked up the language to more clearly communicate its implications to myself and others.

Here's my epiphany: during my junior high and high school years, despite all those classroom-sanctioned reading assignments, I was a reader. And remained so throughout those many years. A closeted reader, certainly, but an engaged reader nevertheless. From my perspective today, I can say I actually loved the act of reading. Tackling one book after another was for me what Louise Rosenblatt describes as "an event." Here's how it went, in short: my middle and high school English teachers assigned a work of Classic Literature (say, for instance, Guy de Maupassant's short story "The Necklace") and I'd read the thing, grudgingly, take and pass the quiz, or write the summary, or compose a literary analysis.

But before the opening bell, during lunch, or after school I headed to the library, where I perused the spines of books, much like author David Rice has advised countless groups of adolescent readers over the years, beginning on the left side of the topmost shelf, working my way down until a title or author's name struck me as interesting. One such book for me was *Stories from El Barrio* (Freedom Voices, 2006) by Piri Thomas.

For me today, looking back on that moment, that book, that event, the initial appeal is obvious: simply, it was the word *barrio*. This was the first time I'd ever encountered Spanish in a title of a book housed in my library filled with nothing but books in English. I removed the book from the shelf, sat on one of the giant beanbags, and read. Read stories like "The Konk" and "Blue Wings and Puerto Rican Knights," and found myself spell-bound by that certain something Rosenblatt refers to as transaction, wherein reader and text come together and out of that interaction a personal meaning is created for the reader. In other words, I saw and heard myself in the characters and stories in this book. I wasn't then, nor am I now a Puerto Rican kid growing up in New York City, but man, if those Latino characters weren't telling my very own story in my very own language, there wouldn't be a character in the world of books who could. Not the way Thomas and his characters were doing it. And my authentic reading career was kept alive in this very way: hidden from teachers, hidden from friends, hidden from family. And what a shame that I felt I had to read in the shadows.

Though what I was getting in the classroom was an even greater shame because it consisted of teachers assigning material boring to me, therefore unengaging, which today leads to the greatest shame of all: that more educators than not know by now a solution to certain illiteracy and aliteracy, and yet they insist on taking part in perpetuating this ill on our young adults. We can't claim ignorance anymore.

And so now we get to the reason for such a book as this one: to do our part as publishers, editors, writers of fiction and poetry both, educators, and best of all, as readers the whole lot of us to help our youth to find a way into the act of reading if they find themselves without, or if already in to stay in it by providing them with stories that are accessible in so many ways.

I first conceived of it years ago when I taught at University of Texas—Pan American. Working with would-be teachers in my Children's and Adolescent literature course—many of them trained in the same way as I had been, for whom reading was a task, something tedious instead of a joy and an event—taught me that ignorance (my own included) begets ignorance. Regarding literacy, if all we are doing is maintaining status quo, then woe to our children who will grow up without ever having experienced the true happiness that reading is.

Back then I talked a good deal about this anthology to Dr. Rob Johnson, who himself had edited an anthology titled *Fantasmas: Supernatural Stories by Mexican American Writers* (Bilingual Review P, 2001), and he was very supportive. Then Dagoberto Gilb's work *Hecho en Tejas: An Anthology of Texas Mexican Literature* (U of New Mexico P, 2006) came out, and though these two books are absolutely necessary in the public school reading and literature classrooms, they differ from this one in that *¡Juventud!* is aimed directly at the younger readership, an audience in the greatest need of good and appealing literature, and make no mistake about it: every story and every poem herein is literature; every bit of it deep in theme, with complicated lines all their own, characters laden with complexity. Stories and poems populated, though, with characters and voices that speak an adolescent's story in his/her own language.

In David Rice's "God's Plan for Wolfie and X-Ray," we meet two boys who mistake violence for manhood, and for whom this discovery turns out to be physically painful. In Myra Infante's "Combustible Sinners," we read about a different sort of journey toward discovery. This one has to do with faith: what it is and how it manifests itself in a myriad ways. "Johnny Quick" by Xavier Garza relates the tale of two brothers who turn bullyism on its head. Rubén Degollado's "A Map of Where I've Been" explores much in the same way as Faulkner does the role family history plays in shaping a boy. David Bowles' fantastical piece, "Oscar and the Giant," tells the story of a boy pushed to the brink and who finds the way through by resting the great weight that life can be on the shoulders of friends, the real giants in that story. "The Noise Expert" by Texas Poet Laureate Jan Seale tells of a young man who goes largely misunderstood and who finds himself on the edge of becoming invisible but for the love and friendship of two co-workers who see his worth beyond the superficial. In Diane Gonzales Bertrand's "The Naked Woman on Poplar Street," we read a story of self-discovery, albeit in a humorous, dare I say, embarrassing way.

Each of these stories has to do with borders in one way or another. Some characters are living on a border, others have crossed over that border, and yet others have crossed the border and returned. Young readers, we hope, will see themselves in any number of these works and therefore recognize the significance of a book like this one. We also hope that educators (administrators, librarians, classroom teachers, and parents) will put this book to good use, that is, by shoving it into the hands of largely text-starved children. Our children.

—René Saldaña, Jr.

My name is Erika Garza-Johnson, and I was the Queen of the University Interscholastic League. In junior high, I participated in a dozen U.I.L. events and even won an award because apparently no one had ever competed in so many events at one time. In high school, more specifically Edcouch-Elsa High School, I had to cut back on my events because I was also a band geek and thus was only able to participate in U.I.L. Ready Writing, Prose, and Poetry. Now, when I was in junior high, I had performed works from the anthology that we used in English, works by poets and writers whose names I don't remember. I did alright, I suppose, maybe even placed 6th. However, my U.I.L. coach for these events in high school, Mrs. Rios, encouraged us to perform something reflecting our cultural background, that being Mexican-American. One of the other students won first place the year before performing a poem by a Mexican-American poet named Carmen Tafolla, who is now the poet laureate of San Antonio. I had never heard of her. In fact, I did not even know that there were books by Mexican–Americans, much less by a Mexican-American woman from Texas. When Mrs. Rios suggested I read *Sonnets to Human Beings* by Tafolla (McGraw-Hill, 1995), I fell in love with her poetry. Written in Spanish and English, it literally spoke to me in ways poetry had never done so before.

You see, I had decided when I was a kid that I was going to be a poet. My father worked for International Paper in Edinburg making cardboard boxes to pack the Valley's fruits and vegetables, and he would bring home reams of paper. I couldn't draw very well, but I could write poems on that paper. I knew that I would never be rich, I knew that I would never be famous—but I also knew that I was going to write poetry anyway. Because I wanted to be a poet, I read whatever poems we were assigned in literature class. I read all of the poems in the anthology edited by Perrine, the book we used in Gifted and Talented English, and then checked out books by the poets I liked and read those. I loved poetry. I was that girl, the one who raises her hand too much and answers all the questions and annoys everyone because I actually read the poems we were supposed to read.

Even though I loved the works in our school textbooks by those, pardon my *Chicana-ismo*, dead white dudes, and even wanted to emulate e.e. cummings and Robert Frost, I couldn't. They weren't like me. They didn't know what it was like to live in a border town. I couldn't take respite in a wooded area on a snowy day; I did not live in a big city like New York. In fact, I had never been outside the Valley. I was raised walking to H.E.B. to call my Granny from a pay phone, I played outside on really hot days that reached 100 degrees, I liked to walk on the railroad tracks and pick up rocks with my dad, and my family spoke English and Spanish. I was a girl from the Rio Grande Valley who wanted to be a poet and I hadn't read anything that reaffirmed that I could be a poet until I read Carmen Tafolla. I never knew you could code-switch, which means to write in English and Spanish, and it is an art all its own. In my junior year of high school I read Sandra Cisneros and Anna Castillo and I learned they were "Chicana" writers like me. After that, I felt I could really write my own experience.

That was 20 plus years ago. Today's youth live in a different time, a different age. They no longer only have access to works that were written 100 years ago that may turn them off to literature altogether. I am, by no means, condemning reading the Western canon; in fact, I believe that students should read all types of literature, beginning with the Classics. I am, however, grateful that I was given the opportunity to collect poetry for a book that students in this region can relate to and that they can discuss and analyze and which will, hopefully, inspire them to write about this place and read, read, read more works that reflect where they are growing up, works that make them feel they, too, are on the literary map.

When I chose the works for *¡Juventud!*, I was looking for poems that painted pictures, shared emotions, and described experiences that could only be written by someone who has lived here and recognizes that there is a well of poems and stories in the Valley that may be unique but that are also universal. I wanted to challenge our youth to let their home be their story and the border be their metaphor. Listen to your parents, your aunts and uncles, listen to your grandparents' stories. Listen with new ears. If you move away or go and travel and see the world, remember who you are and where you come from. You don't have to be Chican@, you don't have to identify with Hispanic or Latino, you can call yourself American, Mexican-American, Valluco, anything you want to. However, while you are here...

Take off your shoes
stick your toes in the fertile soil
go out to the country and listen to the *caña* whistle in the wind
note the orange hue of sorgo like sunset
look up at the palm trees glistening in the Spring sun
framed by fuchsia blossoms on the bougainvillea
inhale the perfume of the citrus orchard
    as it sweetens the air on an early March morning.
Eat your Tiger's Blood *raspa* in the June gloaming,
    listen to the *chicharras*, the mockingbird, the starling sing.
Imagine all the generations before you
    who have seen these images and heard these sounds.
Let your ancestors speak in the southeasterly wind
    blowing off the Gulf of Mexico.

This is your home, carry it in your heart.

There's something magical here, but for me to see this in reality, it helps to read the imaginative works of our local writers, such as those featured in *¡Juventud!* Enjoy this book, discuss it, analyze it, but when you are done reading, look around. Look at this place where you live, and maybe you, too, will see a poem, a story, a song.

—Erika Garza-Johnson

STORIES

God's Plan for Wolfie and X-Ray
by David Rice

THE 80S CULT MOVIE *REPO MAN* WAS THEIR INSPI-
ration for the perfect crime. Wolfie and Ray were
in their comfortable positions, in the living room
three-piece sectional sofa, like two pigs in a pen
lying in cool, damp mud. Wolfie held the remote
control to the T.V. and flipped through the
channels. And then X-Ray shouted, "Hey, stop, go back."
Wolfie, without much response, changed the channels.

"There, stop. This movie is so cool," X-Ray said with
excitement.

"Yeah, what makes it so cool?" Wolfie said, not sharing
X-Ray's enthusiasm.

"Well, it's got these two dudes and their names are the
Rodríguez Brothers and they drive this cool 1964 Ford Falcon
Convertible. They don't even make them anymore."

"How do you know it's a 1964 and not a 1965 Ford
Falcon?" Wolfie asked.

"Hey, one year makes a big difference, and besides, my *tío* has one and he's really cool. He's the one who made me watch this movie," X-Ray said as he nodded.

"Okay, so what's it about?" Wolfie asked mildly interested.

"They're Repo Men, you know. They go around and steal your car if you don't make the payments."

"Awww man, that sucks."

"Yeah, it does, but it's still a funny movie," X-Ray said, and so Wolfie tossed the remote control to the side and they watched the movie.

They were particularly moved by the store robbery scene. Three kids go into a store armed with shotguns and take what cash there is. *"Fácil,"* X-Ray said with the snap of his fingers. "That's not hard, we can do that." Wolfie nodded in agreement with a big smile.

Each could see what the other was thinking, not because they had been friends since they were four, but because everyone in town could see. It was as if they had transparent skulls and all the folks of Edcouch, Texas, could see their nerve impulses speeding through their neurons and jumping with a flash of light from one synaptic function to another. A string of blinking lights tangled around their tiny gears that spun in every wrong direction.

The idea of robbing a store was easy to them because in their blinking minds they had experience in thievery. When they were eight years old they staked out the town cotton gin, and when it was dark enough to see, but not to be seen, they took an old army canvas tent, which X-Ray's father had stolen from the National Guard, and went down to the cotton gin and stuffed it full of cotton.

And then they returned to Wolfie's house and filled a cardboard refrigerator box that Wolfie's father had gotten from the Sears store. Then they took turns jumping into the box from their tree house. All was going well until Wolfie got his wiener dog, Chorizo, and dropped him into the cotton-filled boxes, breaking one of his legs. Wolfie's mother gave them a lecture on the consequences of their actions and how God has a plan for everyone.

"Look, because of what you two did, now Chorizo is suffering. Everything any of us does has consequences. Wolfie, I don't know what God has planned for you, but I'm going to do my best to make it come true."

The next day she took them both to the cotton gin to return the cotton and so they could personally apologize to Mr. Fields, the manager, but when they apologized, their eyes did not look remorseful.

"Mr. Field, could you please weigh this cotton?" she asked. Mr. Fields weighed the cotton and came up with 23 pounds. Wolfie's mother wasted no time and drove Wolfie to church and made him say 23 "Our Father" prayers. As Wolfie prayed she counted them out loud. "This way you will learn," she said.

When they were ten they broke into an abandoned fruit and vegetable packing warehouse that stored quart-sized tin cans and tin lids. They stole five cases of lids, each case containing 250 lids. It took them the better part of the day before they figured out what the lids were best for, saucer fights.

They practiced throwing them at trees, but it was too easy because trees can't run. What they needed was moving targets, and cats and dogs were never anywhere near Wolfie and X-Ray. So they gathered some other kids from their neighborhood and a couple from the neighborhood across Highway 107, and for two days practiced throwing the saucers until the lids became flying blades.

X-Ray's backyard became the battleground for the first saucer fight. The stinging pain of the flying saucers was no worse than being shot by a BB gun, so they were not afraid to rush each other as they flung saucers at UFO speeds. There were many direct hits, and after a few minutes of the battle, it became apparent that even the best dodgeball player could not escape the deadly accuracy of X-Ray's flying saucers. Guillermo Guerrero became a permanent example of this truth.

Guillermo Guerrero's nickname was Gilly, but after one of X-Ray's flying saucers hit him square in the forehead—blood, gushing down his face, Gilly running home, screaming a high pitched scream and then later to the E.R. to receive fifteen stitches across his forehead, which left a familiar scar—his nickname was changed to Frankie, short for Frankenstein.

X-Ray's parents paid the medical expenses and made X-Ray and Wolfie return the lids, but not before making sure the lids were tin and not aluminum, because X-Ray's father knew a place that paid good money for a pound of aluminum.

When Wolfie's mother heard about the incident, she called the police. She was hoping the police could put the boys in jail for a few hours to give them a good scare. But the police said they couldn't do anything because the warehouse manager did not want to press charges.

When Wolfie's mother realized that the police were not going to help, she prayed to the saint of vengeance, St. Michael, for help, and his sword was swift. The good saint's punishment fit the crime. Wolfie, who was an altar boy at St. Theresa Catholic Church in Edcouch, was to serve thirty masses in a row, two masses for every stitch Gilly had received, and had to call Frankie by his Christian name, Guillermo.

When they were thirteen years old, Wolfie and X-Ray were both shot in the backside while stealing oranges from Mr. Gribbens's orchards, but it was only rock salt, and they were far enough away that it only felt like bee stings.

Wolfie's mother ran a tub of cool water and gently helped him in and took a small delight each time she poured a cup of water on his back. "*Ay*, it's stinging," Wolfie said in pain.

Now at sixteen both were more mature, and after viewing hundreds of robberies on television and being dedicated viewers of any and all reality cop shows, they knew they had learned from the mistakes of others. Their hold-up would be flawless.

It was three weeks away from Halloween, and this would give them a perfect excuse for a disguise. Both Wolfie and X-Ray owned a couple of twenty-gauge shotguns. Wolfie's father got his son a shotgun shortly after X-Ray's father bought X-Ray one for his fourteenth birthday. Wolfie's mother protested vehemently, but her husband said that owning a shotgun would teach him responsibility.

After two years of hunting rabbits and whatever else moved, they became good hunters and sure shots, something X-Ray's grandmother would attest to, with all the rabbits and birds she had cooked for them.

Most of their spare time went into planning the store robbery. They scouted out the stores of the surrounding small towns where neither of them had relatives. Their evenings were spent walking into small stores, buying Cokes and candy bars and making mental maps of the store layouts. They checked for T.V. cameras and rented movies with robbery scenes.

Every day they played out the robbery in their heads. Knowing that sometimes robbers would accidentally call each other by their real names, Wolfie and X-Ray gave themselves crazy names, Psycho and Killer, so the store clerk would think twice about trying to take them on.

It was agreed that they would not use real shells during the robbery. Neither was too keen on the idea of killing someone. They decided that the first two shells of their shotguns would be rock salt and the last one would be a live round, to be used only as a last resort, in which case they would aim for a leg or a foot.

After two weeks they picked the Vamos Vete store in the small town of Monte Alto because it was eight miles from Edcouch and eight miles from their hideout. The V.V., as it was called by just about everyone, had no surveillance cameras, and the old man who worked at night seemed easy enough to take. Not to mention the V.V. had fishing equipment they wanted.

At their hideout, an abandoned Airstream International mobile home in the middle of the woods, they dressed themselves as clowns with green hair, and each wore black pants and a black long-sleeve shirt, trying to look as much alike as possible.

Wolfie shouted out, "You ready, Killer!"

X-Ray pumped the shotgun. "V.V., Psycho!"

X-Ray parked his father's truck two blocks away in a field that was behind the V.V., and they walked quietly towards the store as if they were hunting rabbits. Once they got close enough, they darted behind a propane gas tank and peered around it.

Wolfie gave his shotgun to X-Ray and trotted to the corner of the store, then crept along the wall to the edge of the shadow and store lights. He lay down and scooted under a broken-down truck parked on the side of the store. He was equipped with a pen flashlight to signal X-Ray when to move in for the easy action.

After a couple of minutes X-Ray's body beaded in sweat that pushed the clown makeup out from his pores, streaking his sad clown face. His green wig began to make his scalp itch and his leg was falling asleep, and he could hear the mosquitoes calling to their friends, many of whom were feasting on Wolfie.

X-Ray leaned the shotguns against the tank and darted to the corner of the store wall.

"Wolfie. Hey, Wolfie."

Wolfie looked over at X-Ray. "It's Psycho, Psycho!"

"Yeah, yeah. Uh, Psycho, what are you waiting for?"

"Wait for the signal, dude. Be cool, or you're going to mess it up. Get back to the tank and wait for the signal."

"Hurry up," X-Ray said.

X-Ray went back to the tank, and Wolfie knew he had to go with his gut instinct when to make the move, but at the moment his instinct was telling him to forget the whole idea. He looked across the empty parking lot and pointed the pen flashlight toward X-Ray to signal a go.

X-Ray saw the dim light flash, grabbed Wolfie's shotgun and sprinted through the shadow to Wolfie. They both knew this was it because blood filled their chests, and the barrels of their shotguns were no longer cool to their clammy hands.

"*Bueno, idale!*" Wolfie said with a raised voice. The shotguns at their sides, they quickly walked by the store windows. Wolfie glanced inside but did not see any heads over the five-foot shelves. X-Ray swung open the store door and rushed in with Wolfie right behind.

"Okay, old man," X-Ray yelled, "Freeze right there! Don't even get up. Just be cool, man!"

Señor Vásquez, sitting in his blue lawn chair, was startled by the shouts. He dropped the plate of birthday cake his wife had made the night before.

"*¿Qué?* What do you two boys think you're doing? And why are you dressed like clowns?" he asked.

"Because it's Halloween, old man! You just sit and shut up!" X-Ray said with a shove of his shotgun.

"Boys, you don't want to rob this store. There's only forty or fifty dollars in the cash register. Unless you want some fishing equipment, we have lots of that."

"Shut up, old man," X-Ray shouted. "We don't need no stinking fishing equipment! Just what you got in the register."

"Okay, okay. Take the money." Señor Vásquez motioned to the cash register. "But I'm telling you there's nothing in there. Why don't you just take some fishing poles or some baseball caps?"

"I said shut up! Psycho, you get the money and I'll keep an eye on the old man."

Wolfie moved around the counter and made Señor Vásquez get up, while X-Ray kept his shotgun on the old man, who moved slowly while saying, "Okay, okay, take it easy, take it easy."

Wolfie pressed some buttons, but the register let out a continuous beep. Wolfie continued hitting keys, but the high-pitched sound would not cease.

"Hit the no sale button," Señor Vásquez said.

"What?" Wolfie replied.

"He said to hit the no sale button," X-Ray answered.

Wolfie looked at the many keys but couldn't focus on the letters very well since he wasn't wearing his glasses.

"Wolfie, hurry up and hit the no sale button. We don't have—"

"It's Psycho, Psycho! What's wrong with you?"

"Crap! Hey, old man. You didn't hear nothing!"

"What?" Señor Vásquez said as he put one hand to his ear.

"Okay, old man, move!" X-Ray said. "Go help Psycho open the register, and don't try anything, man, or I'll blow your head off!"

Señor Vásquez shook his head and moved toward the cash register, taking it slow because that's how he did everything. Wolfie stood aside and kept his shotgun aimed at the old man.

Señor Vásquez pressed two keys, and the cash drawer sprang with a ring. *"Ahí te va,"* he said.

"Okay, old man. Move away from the register and keep your hands up," X-Ray said.

Wolfie laid his shotgun on the counter, grabbed a paper bag, and began taking the money. His hands were sweaty and his fingers became stiff, making it difficult to grip the bills. It was supposed to be quick, in and out and nobody gets hurt, but he was certain an hour had passed since they'd entered the store.

X-Ray saw the movement from the corner of his eye. Four people walking past the windows.

"Crap! Wolfie, be cool. Old man, act normal and you better be cool." X-Ray ran and hid behind the candy display. Wolfie tried to get down, but it was too late. One had made eye contact with him.

Entering the store were four people in costume: the Lone Ranger, Tonto, Batman and Batgirl. Tonto held the door for the others as they walked in talking and laughing.

X-Ray could see them through a convex mirror in the corner of the store. When all four were in, X-Ray jumped up yelling. "Okay, everybody on the floor! Let's go! On the floor. Move!" He shouted so hard that his voice squeaked.

The Batman let out a short shout and proceeded to dive to the floor, followed by the Lone Ranger and Batgirl.

"Move! Let's go! On the floor, everybody," X-Ray shouted again.

Tonto turned and ran for the door. X-Ray shouted for him to freeze, but Tonto was fast. X-Ray yelled again, but Tonto was halfway out the door. X-Ray pulled up his shotgun and fired. The sound caused Wolfie to jerk and the old man to yell out, "¡Ay, Dios!"

Tonto screamed and arched his back, but didn't stop. He ran past the window in a blur.

"Crap!" X-Ray yelled. "Wolf—Psycho, quick, get the money and let's get the hell out of here."

Batgirl had a feeling she knew the clown's voice, and now she was certain who the robbers were: Wolfie, her first cousin, and his stupid friend X-Ray. With her cape covering her arms, she reached for her bat belt, where she had her mobile phone attached, and began dialing her aunt's phone number. She brought the phone up to her side and then looked up at Wolfie, who looked right back at her.

"I know it's you, Wolfie, and this is your stupid friend X-Ray."

X-Ray pointed the shotgun at her. "Shut up!"

Renée heard a faint hello coming from the phone and knew it was her aunt. She moved the phone away from her side and closer up so her aunt could hear the conversation.

"Wolfie, your mother is going to be real mad when she finds out what you are doing," Renée said. "You just wait. You two are going to get in real trouble for this. Robbing a store. You're so stupid."

Renée could hear Wolfie's mother calling for her husband, telling him to get on the phone so they could both listen.

"I said shut up!" X-Ray yelled. "Psycho, come on, let's go!"

"I wouldn't go out there if I was you, Wolfie. The guy X-Ray shot was Jesús Salvador, and he's a gun nut. He's probably got a bazooka set up so he can blow up your green hair. And why are you guys dressed up like clowns? I mean, what's up with that?"

"Shut up, Renée. Man, *esta* baby can never shut up!" X-Ray said.

"*Ves*, I knew it was you, X-Ray!"

Renée heard her aunt's voice. She was cursing her husband, saying, "You and those damn guns. See what your actions have caused!"

"Would you shut up," she heard her uncle respond. "We have to find out where they are so we can call the police."

Wolfie came around the corner of the counter, making the old man move along as he did. He looked at his cousin and then at X-Ray.

"Come on, let's go," X-Ray said.

"Wolfie, wait," Renée said. "Before you leave, why don't you tell your mother what you're doing?" She slid the mobile phone across the floor to his feet. "She's been listening this entire time."

Wolfie looked at the screen with his mother's picture on it and lowered his arms. X-Ray walked over and stomped on the phone, smashing the plastic box. He grabbed Wolfie by the arm and pulled him toward the glass door.

"That's it! *¡Vámonos!* Time to get the hell out of here!" X-Ray said.

"X-Ray, you're going to pay for that phone!" Renée shouted.

X-Ray and Wolfie stepped outside, and Tonto was behind the old broken down truck. "All right, freeze! Just hold it right there!" He was pointing a gun at them.

X-Ray pointed his shotgun at Tonto. "Drop it!"

"You drop it! Look, there's nowhere to go. I called the police already, and they're on their way, so just forget it."

X-Ray took a tight grip of his shotgun. "Drop the gun or I swear I'll fire!"

Tonto took a tight grip of his gun, though he was shaking too much to get an accurate aim. "I'm not dropping it. You drop it. And besides, Our Lord Jesus Christ will not fail me, and I know all you got in there is rock salt."

"Listen, the rest of the shells are real, and I'll use 'em if you don't drop it," X-Ray shouted.

Wolfie aimed his shotgun, but it was too dark to see anything. X-Ray fired, and Tonto took cover behind the trunk as the rock salt scattered across the metal. Tonto fired back wildly, shattering the store window. Wolfie screamed and X-Ray fired again, this time blasting the truck window. Tonto pulled his gun around the fender and fired aimlessly at Wolfie and X-Ray.

X-Ray was not as fortunate as Wolfie. One wild lucky bullet cut through X-Ray's right shoulder, splitting his shoulder blade into three pieces. He'd be left with a scar and sharp pains every time he tried to do pushups in the state penitentiary.

Wolfie fell to the cement when the other stray bullet went through the inside of his left leg, missing his femur and artery. It was a pain he didn't feel until he heard X-Ray whimpering and moaning about his own wound.

A highway patrol car arrived seconds later. A cop brought out a first-aid kit to help slow the bleeding from the two crying boys. Wolfie's parents came before the ambulance did, and Wolfie's mother held her sobbing son gently in her arms as one of the ambulance crew bandaged his leg.

Wolfie's father stood next to the medic with Renée and Tonto behind him, and asked if his son was going to be okay.

"Hey, he's real lucky compared to that other clown," the medic replied. "If Tonto was a better shot, these two might be dead."

Tonto stepped forward. "Sir, I didn't mean to hurt your son. I'm really sorry. I didn't want to hurt anybody. I was just doing the Lord's work."

Wolfie's mother looked up at Tonto. "What did you say?"

Renée put her hand on Tonto's shoulder and edged forward. "*Sí, tía*. This is my friend Jesús," she said with pride. "He's a criminal justice major at the university, and wants to be a Texas Department of Public safety officer, and he's *also* studying to be a deacon."

Jesús nodded. "Yes. It's true, miss. I'm really sorry about shooting your son, but maybe it's all for the best. I mean, this could be part of God's plan, and this could be a good thing that's happened to your son."

Wolfie's mother held her son and agreed with Jesús.

"Yes, there are consequences and rewards for our actions, and God has a plan for everyone," Wolfie's mother said with firm conviction. "*Mi'jito*, God loves you and this must be part of his plan. It's going to be okay."

A YEAR LATER, WOLFIE AND HIS MOTHER AND FATHER WERE AT church and the mass was as they all were; the constant standing, sitting, standing and kneeling, but it didn't bother Wolfie like it had in the recent past. The pain in his leg was all but gone and only a scar remained which he would often rub through his jeans. After mass Wolfie stayed seated as his parents began to leave the church. Wolfie's father staggered with the crowd, but Wolfie's mother stayed back and saw that her son was still sitting in the pew.

"Are you coming, or what? We can go home now. Church is over: you're free to go," she said.

Wolfie grinned at his mom's little joke, "I know, it's just that it was one year ago today, and I want to say thank you." And he kneeled to pray.

"Really?" his mother asked.

"Yeah, I mean, I could be dead, you know."

His mother smiled and walked back and kneeled next to him. *"Mi'jo,* we have so much to be grateful for." She smiled and closed her eyes in prayer.

Combustible Sinners

by Myra Infante

LISSI SAT ON THE STAGE, WAITING FOR CHURCH TO start. She adjusted her light blue skirt and crossed her ankles, noticing the pantyhose already bunching up around her feet. When she turned fifteen, her mother insisted she start wearing panty hose—she still had to caution Lissi to close her legs so she wasn't showing her underwear. Lissi's father would laugh, reminding her that she didn't want to be like Hermana Gracie, who still didn't know how to sit. Everyone, especially Lissi's father—who as the preacher stood behind the pulpit— knew what color underwear Sister Gracie wore on any given day (usually white on Sundays). Regardless of any weight gain, Sister Gracie insisted on wearing size-ten dresses that would hike up her thighs to cover her considerable width. Lissi looked down at her own skirt to make sure it covered her knees. She hated her dark knees and thought about rubbing them with lemon to make them a lighter shade. She chuckled. *See Mami, I do pray. I have black knees from* *kneeling so much.* Her poor mother would probably use the line as an example of piety at her next meeting with the church ladies.

Before she had left for church that morning, she had seen her parents walk in from the grocery store with grape juice, unsalted crackers, and candles, and she had known that time of the month had come again. At least she wasn't Catholic: Catholics had to take Communion every time they went to church, but they didn't burst into flames if they did so while being unholy.

As she sat on the church stage waiting for people to arrive, Lissi thought about the differences in the sacrament of Communion among churches.

"*Mami*, why do we use grape juice and crackers for communion?" She once asked her mother. "My friend says she eats the white stuff from that candy we get in Mexico. You know…the caramel patties. How come she gets to eat candy during Communion?"

"In the Bible…" her mother began.

Lissi and her sister kept a daily count of how many sentences her mother set up with "in the Bible" or "the Bible says." The record to beat: one hundred and fifty-eight times. Her parents had argued over church members that particular day, and her mother, who had pharisaical tendencies, always consulted the Bible during arguments.

Lissi's mother continued: "…Jesus ordered his disciples to drink of the wine and eat of the bread."

"That still doesn't explain the grape juice and crackers," said Lissi.

"Well, during Jesus' time wine wasn't fermented."

"So why does that wedding miracle talk about drunk wedding guests…you know, the one where Jesus turned the water into wine?"

"*Mira*, Lisita. Grape juice and crackers are the closest we can get to wine and unleavened bread."

That morning, after seeing the paraphernalia for Communion, Lissi rushed over to the Nueva Vida Pentecostal Church, hoping to confess all her sins and be fit for Communion before the service began. Too bad she didn't have a priest to confess to: she would have to wing it on her own and hope however long she prayed prevented her from bursting into flames. Living near church proved perfect for these occasions; she had walked to church by herself since the age of eight. The building had once been a motorcycle shop. Her father had boarded up the garage door with plywood and planned to cover up the large display windows; keeping them clean took too much effort. But Lissi loved those windows. She would spray snow foam on them at Christmas time and string Christmas lights all around them.

Lissi didn't fear an empty church. She would sweep and mop the concrete floors and line up all the folding chairs into rows. An empty church was harmless. Church got scary when *evangelistas* came to preach. They would jump and shout and send even the *abuelitas* to hell. God only knew what sins grandmas committed these days. One preacher from Odessa screamed louder and louder and became hoarser and hoarser; by the time he finished, he sounded like the voice actors used when they played the devil in movies. Lissi always felt guilty thinking that. *I shouldn't compare the things of God with the things of the devil.* She worried she committed blasphemy, the unforgivable sin. She didn't know the exact definition of blasphemy, but saying a preacher sounded like the devil probably qualified in some churches.

Lissi usually managed to hide from most of the visiting *evangelistas*. They had the habit of calling people to the front, and then they would tell that person's secrets in front of the whole congregation. As she sat on the stage, dreading Communion, Lissi thought about the many evangelists that had stood on this very spot.

"You have anger in your heart!"

"Yes," the person would nod, crying.

"You have not forgiven your father!"

"Yes." More crying with a little bit of shaking.

"You have lustful thoughts of a woman that is not your wife!"

At this point, a second person would break out crying— usually the wife. The entire family would hug and cry together for a long time. They would come to church every Sunday for at least a month after that too.

One time a preacher called Lissi to the front. Her breathing got shallow and the elastic ruffle of her blouse pinched her arms. She ran through a list in her head of everything the preacher could accuse her of. Cheating on her chemistry test. Hoping Carlos didn't like her friend Lila. Dancing in the school musical.

"Come here," the preacher said.

Lissi walked down the center aisle towards the stage. The *evangelista* jumped off the stage and pulled the microphone cord, reaching the front row where people sat.

Lissi stood before the preacher and bowed her head.

Here it comes. Anyone have that hotline for runaway kids?

"God is telling me he wants to give you a gift tonight."

Lissi only half listened; she waited for the revelations to start. *Patty hasn't returned my duffel bag. I don't even have a bag to pack my stuff.*

Lissi started to cry. She could hear her mom start to cry too. The entire congregation started praying louder. She heard an *hermana* shout out, "Thank you, God! Thank you, God!" as she clapped her hands. *They think I'm having a spiritual experience. Boy, will they be disappointed when they hear the truth about me.*

The preacher grabbed her hands and "spoke in tongues," which sounded like gibberish sprinkled with English words.

"Woooooooooooooo!" the preacher shouted. "GOD WILL USE THESE HANDS FOR HIS GLORY!"

Lissi held her hands out without moving, squeezing her eyes shut.

"You see that piano over there?"

The preacher pointed to the piano in the far corner.

Lissi opened her eyes and nodded.

The congregation strained their necks to get a glimpse of the old, dusty piano. Lissi heard people whispering and metal folding chairs shifting around.

The preacher looked directly in Lissi's eyes.

"The next time I come to this place, you are going to be playing that piano."

After making Lissi practice for an hour a day with little improvement, her father enrolled her in keyboard lessons. It took a few months for Lissi to learn the chords to the most popular church songs, but her father liked to tell people that she received the gift of playing the piano when the evangelist prayed for her.

And, so, Lissi found herself on the stage behind the new electric piano on this Sunday morning, waiting for God to smite her the minute the grape juice touched her lips because of her latest sins: attending a Catholic *quinceañera*, dancing, and breaking her purity vow.

At the *quinceañera*, all her friends had divided into couples, leaving Lissi all alone. An older boy had started talking to her and had asked her to dance. After the third dance, the boy had tried to kiss Lissi. Despite all the promises she had made God, Lissi continued dancing with the boy and by the fifth dance, she had returned his kiss.

During her own *quinceañera*, Lissi had made a purity vow and expected her first kiss to be during her wedding ceremony. She had read the story in *Christian Youth* magazine of a girl who did just that. The bride and groom smiled happily in the pictures of their honeymoon slash missionary trip.

God had spared her too many times before. Now, her purity ring mocked her, reminding her that taking Communion in such a filthy state would only bring the wrath of God on her.

At least her grandfather had made her laugh that morning after she had seen her parents come in from the grocery store with the items for the piety test known as Communion. When he saw Lissi's parents filling up the little Communion cups with grape juice he said, "*N'ombre, mi'ja.* The first time I heard about the *Santa Cena* I was about your age. *Qué* Holy Supper *ni qué nada.* When my mother called me to supper, I told her, 'No, Ma, the church is serving supper tonight. I'm gonna eat there.'"

Her grandfather chuckled.

"Imagine my surprise when I realized that *Santa Cena,* which I thought meant Holy Supper, was really Communion. It was the smallest supper I had ever seen! *Esto parece cena de bodas,* I thought."

Lissi's grandfather insisted he was a Christian and not a Catholic despite his drinking and smoking. Her mother prayed every night that God would free Grandpa from his *vicios*, but Lissi thought her grandfather's vices made him a lot more fun than her parents.

Lissi smiled to please her grandfather this Sunday morning, but she secretly thought of ways to avoid the entire sacrament. Maybe if she stayed with the children in Sunday School, no one would miss her.

The church service would begin soon and she stood to push the button on her electric piano that made it sound like an organ. She played a few notes. *This sounds ominous enough.* She felt someone tap her shoulder.

"Little Joe wants to know if you have to be baptized to take Communion," her friend Maris said.

"Yes," Lissi hissed and furrowed her brow. "I think the entire church would get into trouble if he took it without being baptized!"

"We would? With who? Your dad?"

"What? No! Not my dad…with GOD…I think…I don't know for sure, but something bad would happen."

"Okay, I'll tell him."

Little Joe was only eleven and unlike the Catholics, the Pentecostals didn't baptize their children until they were twelve.

"How can an infant choose to follow Jesus?" her father always asked during christenings.

Lissi continued playing her bleak tune on the keyboard and realized she didn't have much of a choice about baptism at twelve either. Even as a preteen she had understood that if she delayed her baptism, her parents would think she harbored evil sins in her heart. Usually baptisms were held during Easter, but the year Lissi turned twelve, her father, pleased with the growing numbers of new converts, decided to hold baptisms in November. Lissi hadn't had time to make her peace with God. She had planned to add prayer and Bible reading to her New Year's resolutions, hoping that by the time Easter came, she would have made some considerable points with God. Instead, her father only gave her one week to prepare. As she had waited her turn to be dunked into the small swimming pool hidden behind the curtains, she had paced up and down.

The church youth leader at the time had had a bad boy reputation in his day, but found *la religión* when he met the hottest girl in school. The girl happened to belong to a devout Christian family, and so he turned in his leather jacket for a sports coat and tie. He alone caught glimpses of Lissi's internal turmoil and thought it hilarious to tease her about it.

"Hey, Lissi," she heard her youth leader say as she waited her turn to be baptized.

"Hey, Martin."

"You nervous?"

"A little," she said as she practiced holding her nose and wrist in the customary baptism pose.

"Relax. What's the worst that could happen? It's not like the water will sizzle as you step in. That would only happen if you're like...*evil* or something."

Lissi stopped pacing, and all the blood in her face dropped to her feet.

Martin laughed. "I'm kidding!" He walked away to tell his wife, the hot girl who had converted him, what he had told Lissi. She could see Martin's wife slapping his arm and scrunching up her face. She looked at Lissi, twirled her finger over her ear and pointed to Martin. Lissi laughed. Martin was crazy.

The water didn't sizzle when Lissi was dunked, but then again she had only been twelve back then. God must have still considered her a child; children got a free pass to heaven. *Damn! Sorry, God.* She wished she'd known she held a free pass all that time. As a child, she had tortured herself with thoughts of being left behind during the rapture. She kept listening for the trumpet that announced Jesus' return. At night, she'd sleep with her hand on her sister to make sure the other girl hadn't flown up to heaven in the rapture. She eventually realized her sister had even less of chance of making it to heaven and that she should come up with a better plan than sticking to her as she slept.

Lissi's thoughts returned to her present Communion dilemma. She continued playing arpeggios on the electric piano as people started to fill up the chapel.

"Elizabeth!"

"I want you to play '*Pecador Ven al Dulce Jesús*' right before Communion."

"*¿Esa, ma?*"

"Just do it, Lissi. People have to repent of their sins. Do you know where the candles ended up?"

Lissi ran to the back room to find the candles. By the time she returned, people were already lining up along the stage, waiting for Communion. Lissi stood behind all the people, hoping she would get lost in the crowd. She started placing the candles in their cardboard wax catchers.

Her father began with the warning as usual.

"Whoever, therefore, eats the bread or drinks the cup of the Lord in an unworthy manner will be guilty of profaning the body and blood of the Lord. Let a man examine himself, and so eat of the bread and drink of the cup. Remember, brothers and sisters, that if you have committed any mortal sins for which you have not asked God for forgiveness, you should abstain from taking Communion. What are mortal sins, you ask? Any serious sin would be considered mortal. Murder...participating in an abortion...engaging in homosexual acts...engaging in sex outside of marriage or in an invalid marriage...having impure thoughts...lying...stealing...."

The list went on forever. The deacons walked around with silver trays carrying pieces of crackers and miniature plastic shot cups of grape juice; the brave who had purged their souls of sin took a juice and a piece of cracker. Lissi tried to make herself smaller so no one would notice she didn't grab a cracker and juice. She handed Maris the bag of candles, motioning her to pass them out.

"For anyone who eats and drinks without discerning the body eats and drinks judgment upon himself," her father continued.

She looked up to see her mother staring at her. Her mother's eyes bore into Lissi, motioning her to hurry up and grab the sacrament. Lissi lit her own candle with a match and shared her flame with the person next to her. She scooped up a grape juice and cracker with her free hand as the deacon walked by her.

"Jesus said, 'This is my body.'"

People placed the crackers in their mouths.

Isn't that like cannibalism?

"This is my blood."

And vampirism?

Resigned to her fate, Lissi gulped the miniature shot of grape juice and swallowed the bit of cracker. She closed her eyes and waited for it to burn her insides like acid. Everyone would know her as a fraud now.

Lissi heard a scream from the *hermana* standing in front of her.

Is my face melting off?

Lissi touched her face and opened her eyes.

"¡Me estoy quemando! ¡Me estoy quemando!" screamed the *hermana.*

Lissi's candle had dripped wax on *Hermana* Chanita. Unfortunately, part of *Hermana* Chanita's back was exposed because she wore an almost sexy dress. *Hermano* Roberto splashed his grape juice on Sister Chanita, then grabbed her juice and threw it on her as well. The miniscule Communion cups only managed to stain her dress. She grimaced and groaned, looking back trying to see the damage. *Hermano* Roberto hurriedly peeled the soft wax off of her back, rubbing the red marks the wax had made.

Lissi sat in silence as the service came to a close.

On their way out, Brother Roberto and Sister Chanita walked over to a frazzled Lissi.

"Ay, m'ija, don't worry! I'm fine!" said the *hermana* as she hugged Lissi.

Hermano Roberto caressed the spot where the wax had fallen on the sister and she giggled.

During lunch Lissi's mother said to her father, *"Ay* honey, did you notice *Hermano* Roberto and *Hermana* Chanita didn't take Communion?"

Brother Roberto, a sixty-year-old widower, escorted Sister Chanita, a forty-year-old divorcée to church. Their budding romance had fueled the gossip at church for months.

"I bet you they're back visiting motels again," Lissi's mom said. "I wish they would just get married already."

Well, at least Lissi wouldn't experience damnation on her own. She liked *Hermano* Roberto and Sister Chanita. They would make nice company wherever they all ended up. Why did she always like the sinners the most?

Johnny Quick

by Xavier Garza

WHEN IS COCO LOCO GOING TO GET HERE?" asks my little brother, Johnny, for the seventeenth time. "We've been waiting for hours."

"We've only been waiting for like fifteen minutes," I tell him. Patience has never been one of my little brother's best virtues.

"I hate waiting," he mutters. "I want him to get here now!" That's my little brother...not one ounce of patience in his whole pint-sized body.

"Just make sure that you stick to the plan and be ready."

"I'll be ready," he assures me. "I was born ready!"

A dozen kids have already gathered on the church plaza. Among them are Joe and Martin, the hefty Corona twins. These two brothers are identical in every way save for the fact that one of them wears glasses that are as thick as the rims of a Coca Cola bottle. Their cousin Juanito—aka *the human toothpick*—is here too. He is called the human toothpick because he is super skinny. Jessie from my math class is here, too, as is his younger sister Lucy. We all stand gathered in waiting for the imminent arrival of Coco Loco, the host of a very popular local children's television show. His face is always concealed by white clown make-up accentuated by a mess of unruly, ruby-red yarn hair kept in place by a coconut-shaped helmet.

Nobody knows who Coco Loco truly is. Some say that he is a retired dentist from Monterrey with a great love for children. Still others claim that Coco Loco is not really one person, but rather a group of people who take turns donning the colorful clown make-up. The one thing that is known for sure is that every *Día de los Niños*/Day of the Children, Coco Loco will hop aboard a small airplane and deliver presents wrapped in gold paper adorned with colorful pink or blue ribbons meant for the children in our town. We all jump, waving our arms to catch Coco Loco's attention as he flies overhead. When he sees us, he literally drops presents for us from the sky. These presents we all know are filled with a virtual potpourri of delights that include such goodies as candies, clothes, school supplies, bilingual picture books, and best of all, toys!

"The Ortiz sisters are here," says Johnny. There is a hint of apprehension in Johnny's voice...not that I blame him. Don't let the fact that the Ortiz sisters are girls fool you. Zulema, Marina, Patricia, and Maya Ortiz are infamous for playing rough. Even the school bully knows better than to mess with them. Our cousin Leo had his arm broken once just because he didn't want to be Zulema's boyfriend. She didn't break his arm outright. She is too smart for that. She tripped Leo as he was running down the bleachers at school during gym class. She claimed that Leo had tripped over her foot by accident. All of her friends who were in the same gym class, of course, backed up her story. She even claimed that it was Leo who had wanted them to be boyfriend and girlfriend. "Leo just got mad because I told him that he was too ugly for me to ever like him."

"They always get all the presents," says Johnny.

"It doesn't matter," I tell Johnny. But he does have a point. The last three years the Ortiz sisters have been dominant. Through their combined efforts they have walked away with virtually all the goodies. But this year is going to be different. I have a plan. And the key to my plan's success is my brother Johnny. My little brother is small for his age, but he's quick like a road runner. He has the fastest feet in the fifth grade. My coach is chomping at the bit for little Johnny to get to middle school. "When that happens, we are going to blow all the other school districts out of the water," he tells me. Coach even has a nickname picked out for him already: **JOHNNY QUICK**.

The name fits my little brother to a tee, and I know that if I can just get one of those presents into my little brother's hands nobody will be able to catch him.

"Coco Loco is coming," cries Johnny as he catches sight of Coco Loco's plane.

Coco Loco waves at us from the air and drops four tightly-bound bundles with small parachutes attached to them. The minute the packages hit the ground the Ortiz sisters are on them. By sheer force and intimidation they secure two out of the four packages. Even the hefty Corona twins fall victim to them when Marina trips Joe as he is running, sending him crashing into his brother Martin. A third package lands right between me and Zulema. We both go for it, but I am quicker.

"Give it to me!" screams Zulema. Her sisters hear her and turn their attention towards me.

"Where are you, Johnny?" I cry out as I look around for him. But Johnny is nowhere to be found. I start to run as fast as I can, but I don't even take five steps before Zulema tackles me to the ground. Her sisters begin to pile on top of me one after the other.

"Hand it over," screams Johnny. Seemingly out of nowhere he appears and pulls the package from my hands and begins to run for home. I have seen Johnny run hundreds of times but never as fast as he is running right now. I watch in awe as he expertly zigs and zags his way past anybody who tries to bring him down. Nobody can touch him...not the Ortiz sisters...not the Corona twins...**NOBODY**!

Rising back up to my feet, I chase after him. Johnny keeps running without looking back once. All the kids give up on chasing Johnny except for the Ortiz sisters: they are determined to bring him down. But try as they might, they can't get close to him. He is running so fast now that his feet seem to not even touch the ground! He doesn't bother to stop and open the front gate to our yard either; instead, he leaps over the fence! He does, however, stop long enough to stick his tongue out at the winded Ortiz sisters who are collapsing to the ground as they peer at him from behind the fence. The intimidating presence of our barking German Shepherd *Chato* keeps them from chasing him into our yard.

I follow Johnny to our room and watch as he crumbles atop our bed. His chest heaves up and down wildly.

"Johnny Quick! Johnny Quick!" I begin to chant. "We did it!" We both stare triumphantly at the present on the bed.

"Open it," says Johnny.

"You open it," I tell him. "You earned it."

Johnny tears away the remains of paper and pink ribbons that cling to the cardboard box. He empties out its contents on the bed.

"Dolls?" he questions.

"Pretend make-up kits?" I add.

"A set of jacks?" we both question.

We stand dumbfounded. I had gotten the wrong package! I got the one meant for girls. In retrospect, the pink ribbon should have been a dead giveaway.

"Who got the other package?" I ask Johnny frantically.

"I saw Lucy with it," he tells me. "She sneaked off with it when everyone was jumping on top of you." Lucy is in my brother's class.

"Lucy lives just up the street from us right?" I ask.

"Yes, and I do recall that her package did have a blue ribbon tied to it," says Johnny. "Let's tape the present back up and go to her house," he tells me. "I'm sure she will be willing to trade."

We reassemble the tattered remains using duct tape and begin to head out only to find that the Ortiz sisters are waiting for us. They apparently had figured out our little mix up and are now waiting for us with grins on their faces. I feel panic begin to sink into my heart, but not Johnny. He is already down on one knee tightening the Velcro on his sneakers. He looks up at the Ortiz sisters defiantly.

"Think you can catch me?" he asks them. His words startle all four of the Ortiz sisters.

Johnny stretches his back and does three jumping jacks before grasping the present and dropping to a sprinting position. Looks of doubt etch themselves on the faces of all four of the Ortiz sisters.

"Johnny Quick, Johnny Quick, Johnny Quick," I chant.

"Ready...set...GO**, GO, *GO!*"** screams Johnny as he takes off running like a lightning bolt and leaps over the fence!

The poor Ortiz sisters don't stand a chance. Johnny out runs them all the way to Lucy's house and then back...

The Heartbeat of the Soul of the World
by René Saldaña, Jr.

O N THE DAY OF **PD'S FUNERAL, THE SUN BEAT DOWN** on the mourners gathered at the cemetery. A good many of us from the *barrio* were there. A few from the high school marching band were also in attendance. The heat made us all slouch, sweaty and heavy.

PD's family took up the two rows of chairs directly in front of the coffin, the lid closed for the sake of PD's mother. She had cried and cried when she heard her boy was dead. Just another night out with friends, on his way home, the officer told her. He'd got in a wreck. The other driver'd been drinking. Somehow PD's right arm had been cut off cleanly just below the elbow. His face and head misshapen but without a bruise or scratch. This last part the cop didn't tell her. She saw for herself at the morgue.

That night, a few hours after news of the wreck, one of the boys in Peñitas, hiding from his parents on the roof of his house, nearly fell from his perch when he heard PD's mom screaming out her dead son's name: *"Ay, mi Pedro, mi*

Pedrito. Ay, Diosito Santo. ¿Porqué, Diosito?" The boy thought it was *La Llorona* crying out for her drowned babies, and that's when he almost fell.

Today at the funeral, PD's mom was all cried out. All she did was grab at her chest and moan, wrinkle her face, moan some more. Times like these—the heat oppressive, your son dead—what else is there left to do?

Mr. Stevens, the band director, had found a place in the very last row of chairs, not covered by the canopy. He was wearing dark sunglasses and his green tweed jacket, and he'd trimmed his scraggly red-blond beard. He was older, maybe forty-five, maybe fifty, and scrawny. He looked like he was carrying the load of the world on his skinny shoulders. He looked beaten.

Mr. Stevens had been hired on as an assistant director at the high school six years back, and when the old band director retired, he took over. He loved jazz and the blues, couldn't get enough of the South Texas *conjunto* music since first he'd heard it one Saturday morning on a public radio station, and had all kinds of music playing in his office and over the speakers in the band hall when class wasn't in session.

One day three years ago, frustrated by his students' lack of enthusiasm for the piece they were taking to competitions, he stopped a rehearsal midway, pulled out a couple of LPs and a record player from his office, and said to the students, "This it Miles Davis. Listen. It's his heart and soul. He's showing you the world's core through his music. The clay and fire. He's letting you in on its secrets, every one of them. That's how you need to be playing…. Now listen to this. It's Coltrane…." He propped up the LP covers on the chalkboard railing behind him for his students to see.

One kid said, "This is Black music, man. You're a gringo, we're Hispanic. What's it have to do with you? Or us?"

"This isn't Black music. It's not even music. It's beyond music." They all stared at their teacher blankly. "It's hard to explain," he said, "but, wait—wait right here, okay?" He left the hall, and in a few moments returned with a CD. He didn't cut Coltrane off, just turned him down. It was still there, a buzz in the corner by the trumpet section. Then Stevens played Narciso Martinez. "See?" he said after a few moments. "Now do you hear it? The secrets are here, too. Like a heaviness. Can you hear the weight in the music? It's in the *bajo sexto* and the accordion." He closed his eyes and tapped the beat on his chest.

Some of the band members giggled, nervous that their director had lost his mind. The same kid from before said, "You think we're wetbacks, Stevens?" Some more students laughed.

But not PD.

He was still lost on Miles and Coltrane, especially Coltrane, shutting out all the noise: the kid complaining, Melissa next to PD blowing the spit out of her trumpet, Stevens talking, the others laughing. Just Coltrane now,

buzzing somewhere in the corner, a raspy river of sound. Then Narciso and his accordion joined in. PD closed his eyes and imagined Coltrane and Narciso on a stage—
the one a Black guy and the other a Mexican. Just two guys on a dark stage playing a sax and an accordion; then no Coltrane and no Narciso, just their music on the stage. Their sounds swirling together, and an explosion next, then the notes showering down on PD, who was standing in the middle of the stage now, crying and laughing. *How can that happen?* he wondered. The music, its heaviness, in his chest, a slush of tears in there, and laughter.

PD got what Mr. Stevens was saying. Stevens looked at the record player like he could see these same guys on stage too.

"It's about the music," he said, biting at his fingernails. "It's about their souls, *our* souls." He let Narciso play through to the end of the song.

Everyone stayed quiet until the song was over, then Stevens turned it all off. But PD got it stuck in his mind. It played in his ears the rest of the day, all through English II, Algebra I, history, on up to marching practice in the afternoon heat, where he was unable to concentrate on the steps he had already memorized, mucking it up for all of the marching band, forcing them to have to start over.

But Coltrane, man, he got to PD something fierce. And Narciso, too. He began to mix up the sax and the accordion. It was supposed to be Coltrane, his sound; instead, PD kept hearing the same music—Coltrane's, but coming out of Narciso's accordion. PD shook his head, and was somehow able to get through that afternoon's band practice.

Next day, Mr. Stevens heard music down the hall from his office, a trumpet, and for a second he thought it was somebody playing his record from yesterday. He sat on his clunky chair, heavy with the music, almost like he was drowning in a river rushing past. He got up finally, his eyes half closed as he walked, listening to the music. It was Coltrane he heard, but on a trumpet from one of the practice rooms. Stuff he'd heard before but never heard before, not quite like this, if you get what I mean. Harder, maybe like early Coltrane playing his older stuff, but on a trumpet. He walked through the empty hall. Beyond the hall. That's where it was coming from.

He walked to the practice rooms and saw through the glass it was PD, playing his trumpet, his back to the door, his head dipping to a beat.

Stevens imagined PD had his eyes closed, the boy's right knee rising and falling to that same beat. Then it was that Stevens noticed the boy playing the same song over and over, what he'd played to the students yesterday and with it something else mixed in, that harder primal sound—those're the only words he could use to try to explain to himself the boy's playing: hard, base, basic, primal, crude, original, the world's soul exposed. He heard the accordion coming out of this boy's trumpet, and a sax. This boy, third-chair trumpet, a sophomore, good enough at playing and marching, not exceptional, but just good enough. Stevens couldn't understand this boy's playing right now.

Then PD turned, his trumpet on his lap, and looked at Stevens. "Sorry. I should go." PD had decided to skip English II. He began to put away his horn. "What's that you were playing? I mean, I know what it is, but..." He looked over PD's shoulder. "Where's your sheet music?"

"No sheet music. Playing from memory."

"From yesterday?"

The boy nodded.

"But it was such a short moment. You couldn't have—"

"It was long enough. That John Coltrane is good. And Narciso Martinez, also. You wouldn't think that they're so much alike, that they can say the same thing to you, being different like they are. But..."

"Yeah, you wouldn't know it at all. I mean to say, most people wouldn't know it. But you got it."

"I think so."

PD clasped shut his instrument case and left the band hall. Mr. Stevens walked back to his office, all the while shaking his head.

Two or three days later, Stevens loaned several CDs to PD. Some more jazz, some blues, a bit of classical, something that sounded foreign to PD, maybe Jewish. Lots more stuff. But PD didn't have a CD player, so he took one from a teacher's room, and he listened to all the music at home. For a week he kept the player and the music, and he could hardly sleep. Then, before hopping on the bus to go to an away football game with the band that Friday afternoon, he handed back the music to Mr. Stevens. "Thanks," he said. Earlier, he'd snuck back to that teacher's room and replaced the CD player, right where he'd found it.

The following Monday, Mr. Stevens asked PD, "So? What did you think?"

"It's so clear. They're all telling me the same thing."

"What's that?"

"It's about suffering. More than that—the struggle. But the overcoming it too. I could hear the heaviness. It weighs a ton, man."

The two became fast friends. Dig it—an old white dude and a young Chicano kid. Who would've thought? I'm not saying they hung out at lunchtime or dared each other to go steal a soda from the corner store, or talked in secret about their girlfriends. Seeing them in class, you wouldn't even guess they knew each other except for in the band hall, teacher and student. Stevens didn't promote PD to first chair, and PD didn't call Mr. Stevens by his first name, not in private, and definitely not in public. But they were good friends, the best.

PD's senior year, Stevens got PD a gig. That's what he called it, a gig. At some café downtown in McAllen. PD had been working on some of his own stuff this last year—Indio Blues, he called it. That night at the café, Stevens played a bit of the bass guitar—*toam-tum-tum*—a heartbeat that vibrated just underneath the tiled floor all the way to PD's feet, then up his legs and spine; and soon his own heart matched the tempo of the bass.

He was nervous—the lights all on him, his stomach vibrating from Stevens' bass—so he closed his eyes, put his trumpet to his lips, and played. Man, the first set he dragged out for close to a half hour, nonstop. But it wasn't the same song for that long. He'd take a deep breath and change directions, and Stevens had to play catch-up. When PD finished, Stevens stopped—dead cold, in the middle of some riff he was on; but it worked. You know how it is—you come to the end when the end comes. That's that.

PD was exhausted after two more sets just like the first one—sweaty, drooping at the shoulders, but blowing his Indio Blues solid, all the way through to the end.

Then he played every weekend at different places. Stevens backing him up, but most times he'd just quit playing the bass and listen. That's how good this kid was. Nobody cried because of his playing. He didn't bring people to their knees. Nobody fainted. But they heard it was their song he was playing, some people looking around to see if the others knew their secrets were being exposed in the notes. Embarrassed. But every one of them, their hearts in their throats. Happy and sad all at once.

This week, we lost—the bunch of us—we lost something of his music in PD's passing. Each of us some different note of his, but each just as heavy.

This afternoon, Stevens, under his sunglasses, cried. So did PD's family and friends. They cried because he was gone—no more of his early morning practicing on his horn, waking everybody in the whole house, in the entire neighborhood. Stevens cried because he'd heard PD play that first time in the band hall. He'd played behind him at the coffeehouses in town. Now, Stevens heard only the memory of the sound, reverberating, a buzz, the heartbeat of the soul of the world. His shoulders shaking under the load of it all. He cried, wondering if the memory was enough.

This afternoon, at the cemetery, the sun pounded down something fierce. A trying heat—and there was no tent big enough to keep it off us all.

A Map of Where I've Been
by Rubén Degollado

WHEN I WAS A *CHIQUILLO* AND MY PARENTS WERE happier and not drinking so much, Sundays meant church and *Papá* Tavo and *'Buelita* Guadalupe's house. Now, in the junior year of my life, Sundays meant checking out the cars and the girls at Westside Park and afterward driving to my grandparents' house without my parents. Sometimes it was just having lunch with *'Buelita,* her *guisos, mole* or chicken and rice, and always her *tortillas.* Other times there were *pachangas,* parties for my little cousins' birthdays, or get-togethers just because. Ever since my grandfather *Papá* Tavo had had a nervous breakdown and he was in the nursing home at the San Juan Shrine, Sundays also meant going there, too.

This one Sunday, I especially wanted to go to *'Buelita's* because my cousin Erika, *Tía* Marisol and *Tío* Lalo's daughter, was having her second birthday party. Almost all of the Izquierdos were going to be there. Even a few of my *tíos* and *tías* had come down from San Antonio for the weekend. My little cousin Erika was something else. At two, she had attitude walking around with a toy purse and telling us "no" any time we tried to hug her or get some *besitos*. She also danced like Selena any time one of her songs came on the radio or her dad asked her to show how she danced at our *tía* Suzana's wedding.

'Buelita's neighborhood, La Zavala in McAllen, wasn't East Los, and the Zavaleros wouldn't blast you if they didn't know you, but the *locos* still looked at you *gacho* if you didn't belong or they had never seen your car before. The only times they'd mess you up is if you came in throwing colors or signs, just asking for trouble like some junior high wannabe. This was my father's *barrio*, where he used to run around with his brothers, causing panic around town. He was in an old-school gang called *Los* Diggers. Me, they knew I was all Mission, but they also knew who my Pop was and that I was an Izquierdo and that I had been coming there since I was a kid. We'd all seen each other since we were little, me and my cousins walking to Circle K or to play on the swings behind St. Joseph's church. I'd even played with some of them way back then. So I'd drive up Ithaca Avenue in the work truck Pop let me drive and none of them threw me even a sideways glance. Only the younger ones without respect, little junior high *esquincles* trying to act all bad, staring me down as if it would scare me. I had to laugh. They had no way of knowing the things I had seen, the things I had done.

As soon as I rolled up in Pop's old Ford work truck, I could smell the smoke from the barbecue pit. With this smell of mesquite and *fajitas*, with the sounds of my *tíos* laughing, with my *tías* talking inside beyond the burglar bars, with my little cousins running around my legs, I forgot everything that was happening in my life and how my *Papá* Tavo was sick and would not last much longer. People all over the Zavala could smell that barbecue chicken and those *fajitas* coming from 'Buelita Guadalupe's yard and now everyone inside their houses all around the Zavala wanted to cook-out. Ruben's Grocery would be getting some good business soon. I couldn't remember the last time I had eaten *fajitas*. It had been too long since I had come around. I could make excuses and say it was because Mama was mad at 'Buelita for something again or that I had been too busy with my *camaradas*, but these were not excuses. These were failings.

When I walked in, everybody said, "¡Mira, Cirilo!" Everyone was so excited I was there because me, Pop, and Mama hadn't been to 'Buelita's in several months. The last time they had gone, 'Buelita told Pop and Mama they were spending too much time in the bars, not visiting *Papá* Tavo, my grandfather, in the nursing home, and not taking care of me like they were supposed to. You couldn't tell Mama something like that and have her take it. Once you told her anything or did her wrong, forget it. She would never let it go. Even if she did talk nice to you afterward, this thing would always be there, behind her eyes, in the way she said things to you.

My parents hadn't spoken to *'Buelita* since that argument, but they didn't care if I went to her house. Mostly this silence between them was not just because of the argument, but because of the *sangre pesada* between Mama and *'Buelita*. They'd never gotten along. Before they got married, Pop messed up by telling Mama what *'Buelita* had told him about her. *That woman, she is going to be very expensive*, *'Buelita* had said. Mama had never really forgiven *'Buelita* for saying that. With the way Mama bought gold jewelry all the time, and had her hair done by her hairdresser Benny for fifty or sixty dollars, and her nails done by the *chinitos* downtown, *'Buelita* had pretty much been right. Anyway, if my parents ever got mad that I was here at *'Buelita's*, I'd still go. They couldn't stop me. I should have come before this. At least it was a birthday and not somebody dying that made me come around.

I went into the kitchen where some of my *tíos* were cutting more *fajitas*, laughing with pink meat and fat in their hands. The Three Amigos Gordos everyone called my uncles Lalo, Manuel, and Joe because of their beer bellies. They held out the meat in front of my face. My *tío* Manuel gave me his elbow to shake since his hands were full. My *tío* Lalo laughed his big belly laugh, said, "Good to see you, *mi'jo!*" and patted me on the back in his rough way. When I was smaller and he used to do this, it almost knocked me down.

Now, at sixteen, I could stand up without losing my balance. I was getting taller than all of my *tíos*, even though everyone said I was so skinny I looked like a *palo* standing next to them.

Tío Gonzalo shook my hand, smiled, and took a plate of raw chicken out to the *bote de basura*.

My *tías* were all sitting at the table, drinking wine coolers and some drinking coffee, even though it was so hot, especially in the kitchen where there was the pot of *charro* beans on the stove.

I bent and kissed my *tías* on the cheeks, one by one. When I got to *Tía* Marisol, I said, "*Tía*, are you losing weight?" I said this every time I saw her, but it was never true. She was good to me, and it made her feel better. Any time she saw me, she didn't say things like *Long time no see, stranger,* or *Where have you been?* She didn't judge or give me the evil eye because of what my parents had done. My *tía* Marisol was just happy to see me.

"*Ay, mi'jo, gracias* for noticing. I'm on *ese* low-carb diet where I can eat a lot of meat and bacon and *barbacoa*, but no bread or *tortillas*. Why don't you tell your *tío* I've lost weight, *mi'jo*? He don't seem to notice." She said this last part, pointing her eyebrows at *Tío* Lalo who was chopping at the chicken, cutting it down the middle and laughing the whole time.

"*Oye, Tío*, have you noticed my *tía's* losing weight? She's looking fine. You better watch out the next time you go to a dance." All my *tías* laughed and *Tía* Marisol said, *"Ay mi'jo*, you're crazy."

Tío Lalo patted his own big, hairy *panza*. "Hey, *vieja*, look right here. *Mira. ¿Sabes qué?* You can never leave my beauty. *Aquí te tengo* under my power."

"Power, *ni qué* power."

I looked around for *'Buelita*, but I was sure she wasn't in the room since *Tío* Lalo would never do anything like that in front of her. He loved and respected *'Buelita*, his *suegra*, as much as his own mother. I also looked around for my *tía* Victoria, my *tío* Gonzalo's new, younger wife. If my friends saw her, they would say she was *bien buena*. She was another reason I liked to come around. Who doesn't like to talk to a pretty woman? At twenty-seven and as good looking as she was, she could have gone cruising with us and no one would have thought anything about it except that we'd done good for ourselves.

"Where's *'Buelita*?" I said.

"She's in Suzana's room. Go say hi, *mi'jo*; she'll be happy to know you're here."

When Suzana got married to this little Mexican national named Artemio who used to be a horse jockey, she moved out of her room at *'Buelita's*. Then, *'Buelita* turned Suzana's room into a place to pray, like a mini-version of the San Juan Shrine *del Valle*. This was around the same time *Papá* Tavo went into Charter Palms for going crazy whenever there was a full moon. With my grandfather out in the yard looking for buried black magic curses and yelling at the top of his lungs in the middle of the night, what else could she do but say it was okay to put him there, and pray and pray that he would get better?

After Charter Palms, his liver got sick from all the medicine he was taking. Then, he moved from nursing home to nursing home, to the place where he was now, San Juan Nursing Home at the San Juan Shrine. 'Buelita also prayed because she was afraid. She would call my pop or my tío Gonzalo or Lalo in the middle of the night so they could come check around the house. She said bad kids in the neighborhood were always crossing through her yard, looking into windows for something they could steal. Whenever Pop or one of my tíos got there, they never saw anything, any gangsters, or any sign the gangsters had been there. This was also another reason why Mama didn't like 'Buelita. She thought 'Buelita did it for attention.

There was a little black and white T.V. screen in the living room. It had four different pictures, and as I looked closer, it was four different angles of her yard.

"Pobrecita," I said to myself. The T.V. screen was hooked up to surveillance cameras Tío Gonzalo had installed outside. I imagined 'Buelita sitting there at night, next to the phone, just waiting to see some kids jump the fence. It made me want to hurt those little Zavaleros. I mean what kind of barrio was it where kids from the neighborhood were trying to steal things from an old woman in the same neighborhood? Messed *up*. It was never supposed to be this way, even though I'm sure it also happened in Mission where we lived.

I heard her whispered prayers. Her prayer voice made me calm like it did during all those Christmases when she prayed the rosary and all I could think about was opening presents.

Her back was to me and she was kneeling down. She could stay that way longer than anyone I knew. I knew this because some Christmases we'd say the rosary inside, on our knees. Us kids shifted from knee to knee because it hurt us so much, but *'Buelita* would be there, not moving at all, her eyes shut tight, her spirit somewhere far away from us, whispering every bead. Once, inside the church at San Juan, after all of us had visited *Papá* Tavo, she had walked on her knees all the way from the back to the altar in the front. All the way, on her knees.

At the top of her altar was a framed picture of the *Virgen de Guadalupe*, the one that you see on Rollin' Low T-shirts and lowriders, the one where she's wearing the blue cape with twelve stars on it and the half-moon under her brown feet. *'Buelita* also had this big wooden rosary hanging, the crucifix as big as a hammer, the beads as big as pecans. There was also this picture of Jesus hanging where if you looked at it from one side, He was kneeling by some rock and if you looked at it another way, He was bleeding, with His sad crying eyes looking up to the Father who didn't help

Him. I used to draw this face all the time, and had even won an art award my freshman year. The drawing I had done was on the wall next to that picture I had copied, along with some of my other cousins' drawings and essays from school. Whenever I looked at it, I wondered why Jesus wasn't mad at His Father for letting Him be killed like that. Sometimes I hated my father for less than that. I guess that was why He was Jesus and I was Cirilo.

I stood there by the open door, watching her, noticing how her ponytail had gotten more white hair in it. I didn't say anything.

"Come in, *mi'jo*," she said without turning. In Spanish, she said, "I want to talk to you."

"How did you know it was me? Did God tell you I would come?"

"No, *mi'jo*, I heard everyone when they said, '*¡Mira Cirilo!*' Also, I heard you driving your father's old truck."

She stayed on her knees for a little too long, like she wanted me to get down on the floor with her, too. I stayed standing by the door.

I felt better when she motioned for me to help her get up. '*Buelita* held out her arms and I gave her my *abrazo*, the kind of tight hug I saved for my grandmother. In Spanish, she said, "How have you been, *mi'jo*? It has been so long since I have seen you."

"*Sí*, '*Buelita*, it's been too long. I've been good."

We were still hugging each other when she said, "*Qué bueno, qué bueno*. It is so good to see you," sounding like she was about to cry. I was glad when she didn't. I could stand to hear anyone else but my grandmother cry, even Mama.

"What I wanted to tell you was I have been praying for you and your father and mother, and I know it is all going to get better. God told me your father is going to change."

What about my mother? I thought, but didn't ask. I just said, "That's good, *'Buelita*, that's good."

"No, *mi'jo*, I know it is good, but you have to believe it. And I am not saying this to make you feel better. I am saying this because I know. But your mother? I do not know."

After a couple hours, when more people showed up, like *Tía* Victoria and *Tío* Gonzalo and Little Gonzalo, they decided to put up the *piñata*. Because I was pretty skinny and didn't weigh that much and was old enough to go on the roof, they asked me to control the *piñata*, a clown with a big balloon stomach, the big kind you bought in Reynosa and not one of those cheap little ones from H.E.B. This was going to be fun, being on the other side of the *piñata*, the one teasing the little kids.

All my little cousins had tried to bust the *piñata* already. I had been good to them, but sometimes *piñatas* were very thick, and no matter how hard they swung the broomstick, the little kids couldn't bust it.

My cousin Seferino, the oldest kid there, was up to bat last, and since he was big enough, he had a blindfold on. Sef looked like a little *Tío* Lalo with those small eyes and that big stomach. He spit on his hands, rubbed them together, and said, "Bring it on, *cachetón*!" Sef swung the broomstick wild and I pulled on the *piñata*. It went rolling through the air, and everyone went, "Oh!" He was swinging wild, not even coming close, and everybody kept moving out more and more because he had a lot of weight behind his swing. Somebody could get *hurt*.

When Sef stopped, I put the *piñata* on top of his head and lifted the clown as soon as he tried to hit it.

Sef said, "*Ya güey*, don't be like that."

Tío Lalo said, "Sef," because he'd said "*güey*" in front of 'Buelita. It was okay for Sef to say it in front of him, just not in front of 'Buelita, even though "*güey*" wasn't that bad of a word. It was like saying "man," but it was a respect thing not saying it in front of people older than you.

Finally, because I could tell everyone was getting bored, thinking, Ya, *let him hit it already, our kids want some candy!* I kept it from moving, and Sef took this big swing. Candy went flying everywhere, but Sef kept going.

All the grownups said, "Wait, wait, *wait*!" but Sef kept on anyway, and Little Gonzalo ran in. You see, when you're hitting a *piñata* or standing around the circle waiting for candy, something takes over you. You can't hear what the grownups are saying. All you're thinking about is busting that *piñata* way open or running and grabbing as much candy as you can. It's like when somebody's getting jumped, and nobody wants to stop, even when the teachers and *chotas* finally show up, break through the crowd and are yelling and pulling you off of each other. It was like so many fights I had seen or been in.

I was above everybody, and I saw it happen all slow-motion before everyone else. The broomstick came back as Sef was going for another swing and—*zas*—my cousin Little Gonzalo's head was there. He was on the ground now and stupid Sef, all crazy with thoughts of candy, couldn't hear all the grownups saying, "Stop! *Stop* it!" Finally, he stopped because my *tío* Lalo slapped him on the back of the head. *Tía* Victoria went to Little Gonzalo. All the kids didn't care. They were making candy bags out of their shirts, holding them out with one hand and throwing candy in with the other.

Tía Victoria was sitting there, and she wasn't treating Little Gonzalo like a baby, even though he was screaming and rolling around in the dirt. She was saying, "It's okay, *mi'jo*, you're all right. You don't need to cry." His head was going to have this big *chipote*, but there wasn't any blood. Little Gonzalo just kept sucking air and trying to bury his face into *Tía* Victoria, saying, "Mama, Mama, Mama." When I saw her face, and her eyes were looking into mine, I felt bad about making Seferino have to work at hitting the *piñata*. Maybe if I'd made it easier, Seferino wouldn't have gone so crazy with the bat. She smiled at me and shook her head as if to say everything was okay.

Tía said, "*Sana, sana, colita de rana, si no sanarás, sanarás, mañana.*" Our mothers say this when we're hurt, but not too bad. It means, *Heal, heal, little frog's tail. If you don't heal today, you'll heal tomorrow.* It doesn't sound the same in English, though. Little Gonzalo would not get up or look at any of us. There was this big red *chipote* on his forehead, like this big avocado pit was growing inside, but he was going to be okay, if he ever stopped crying.

Tía Victoria said, "Go play, *mi'jo*, go play. You're all right. Be a tough little man." She wasn't treating him like that because she didn't care about him, but because she didn't want him to be a mama's boy. Everybody knows mama's boys get jumped, so it was a good thing she didn't baby him. I hoped Little Gonzalo got over this before he went to school, because the first time he did this at school, it would be all over for him. The other kids would knock him down just to watch the show.

Sef went up to Little Gonzalo with his shirt full of candy, his big *panza* showing to everybody, and told him he was sorry. "You want to share my candy?"

Now, we were all sitting down at the table in the kitchen eating. The little kids were in the living room watching a cartoon video someone had put on. I was with all my *tías* and *tíos* eating. We were eating serious, no talking at all. You could hear the sound of ice in our glasses of Coke, the sound of our arms sticking to the plastic cover on the table. Once in a while, someone would ask if there were more *tortillas* and one of the women or girl cousins would get up to heat more *tortillas*.

I was sitting next to *Tía* Victoria, and Little Gonzalo was on her lap. This was the way they were, always talking to each other real quiet, like they were telling secrets, always praying together before they ate. Some of my older cousins like Sef sometimes made fun of Little Gonzalo because he and his mom were so close, and Little Gonzalo cried for everything, but I always stuck up for him. If they messed with him, I gave them *nacas*, the thing I did where I got them in a headlock and hit the tops of their heads with my middle knuckle.

"So, what's up, LG?" I said. "You break any hearts at the preschool yet?"

Little Gonzalo smiled real big.

"*Ay*, Cirilo," *Tía* Victoria said. "Don't encourage him. That boy is pure Izquierdo." She meant that all us boys and men with Izquierdo blood were dogs. We could always get pretty women without even trying too hard.

"Do you know what they caught him doing at daycare?"

"Oh no, *Tía*, what? Being *travieso*?"

"Much worse. *Deja tú*, they found him and this little girl hiding in the *gabinetes* underneath the sink. I said, '*Mi'jo*, your daycare's called Little Friends, not Little Kissy Kissy Friends.' This one's going to be bad. *Va a ser terrible.*"

Little Gonzalo smiled bigger at the word *terrible*.

"Little man knows. Ain't that right, LG?"

"I like girls," Little Gonzalo said, lifting his shoulders and smiling.

"I know you do, *mi'jo*. Just like your father and your uncles and your cousin Cirilo. *Y tú*, Light Eyes? Got any girlfriends?"

Even before she finished her sentence, I thought of Karina. She was *La X*, the *Llorona* who still walked in the night of my dreams, crying out for how she had hurt me, asking for forgiveness. This was in dreams. In life, *La X* acted like she had never known me, like we had never gone around or told each other our secrets.

Tía Victoria didn't need to know about her. "No, *Tía*, I don't."

"*¿Y por qué no? ¿Cómo puede ser?*"

"Better being alone. I can go out with my friends without some girl telling me what to do."

Tía Victoria looked around the table, around the room. Everyone had left. It was just me and her still eating now.

"*¿Sabes qué, mi'jo?* I'm going to tell you something. Those colored eyes of yours, some girl's going to look into them and see there's something special about you. I go to the mall and to Peter Piper Pizza, and I see all these little gangsters, and in a way, they look just like you, *así todos pelones y con sus pantalones bien* baggys. You know those Hispanics causing panic. But, you don't want that life. I see something better for you." Now she sounded like every teacher who said they had cared about me.

"You think so, huh?"

"No, *mi'jo*, I *know* so. I know you've probably heard it all before, but listen. *Tus ojos borrados*, those eyes of yours see things others don't. Why do you think you can draw so good? It's not in the hands. It's in the eyes. You really look deep into things, see how beautiful they are. Like that one picture of Jesus you drew when you were in junior high where He is praying at Gethsemane. You really captured the strength in His face, in His eyes. No wonder you got that award. *Mi'jo*, just keep it up. *Así*, with your art and your words, you just have to share what you've seen, tell everybody what you know. You will one day share the gospel in your own special way."

AFTERWARD, I DROVE OVER TO SAN JUAN NURSING HOME because I was supposed to meet Pop, which was something we did every Sunday. Pop also told me he was going to light a candle at San Juditas in Pharr afterward, and asked me if I wanted to go. Pop went to San Juditas when he had gotten up too late to go to *misa*. It helped him, made him feel like a good Catholic even though the reason he hadn't gone to morning mass was because he was all *crudo* from the night before. I didn't want anything to do with that, but I did agree with Pop that it was important to see *Papá* Tavo.

I walked into the yellow halls and the smell was ugly. This old lady named Margarita was sitting by the T.V. on her big rolling recliner. She was banging the tray like I'd seen her do every time I'd ever visited. If you didn't see Margarita, you could always *hear* her somewhere, knocking the tray with her fists three times, then clapping three times. She'd sit there, her toothless mouth, her empty eyes looking up into space: knock, knock, knock, clap, clap, clap. Every time. If I ever came in and Margarita wasn't doing it, it'd be because she was gone.

I never liked going to the San Juan Nursing Home, but went anyway, out of respect and love for my grandfather *Papá* Tavo. All the older people who went, my *tías* and *tíos*, made their kids go. None of the little ones wanted to be there because the only *Papá* Tavo they knew was this sick old man in a nursing home, the one who only talked to us sometimes when he was having a good day. Other days, *Papá* Tavo didn't even know who we were, or he just asked us for cigarettes we couldn't give him.

Pop was sitting by the bed, combing *Papá* Tavo's hair, doing it real slow making sure not to scratch his head. Even though *Papá* Tavo's mind and body were dying day by day, he had this real long, gray *greña* that kept growing long no matter what. Why didn't anyone at the nursing home ever comb his hair? His fingernails were the same way, growing and growing and growing.

The *Papá* Tavo lying there—his thick fingernails like wood, his mouth open, his eyes staring out the window, his skin loose like a paper bag, him not saying much of anything we could understand anymore—was the only *abuelo* my little cousins had ever known. Too sad for them.

They couldn't remember him going downtown on 17th Street to play dominoes, how he would buy us something from the ice cream truck whenever it came by: ice cream sandwiches, push-ups or drumsticks. They couldn't know *Papá* Tavo at the kitchen table, showing me and Sef and my cousin, Dianira, how to play dominoes, ice cream dripping all over the pieces and *Papá* Tavo not even caring, just laughing with us. The only way they could know this *Papá* Tavo was from pictures, the grandpa that danced *cumbias* with 'Buelita at weddings and *quinceañeras*, his Stetson hat tilted at a cocky angle, back when he still had muscles on him.

Why was this strong man taken from us? Some in the family say it was because he had a nervous breakdown because of being worried that he would not be able to feed all of his children, that he would have nightmares about our *tíos* and *tías* begging him for milk he could not buy. Others say he was cursed by a man across the street named Emiliano Contreras who was known to be a *brujo*, a bad man who made black curses against people he hated or was jealous of. Supposedly this man Contreras did all kinds of *hechizos* against my family, the Izquierdos, because of *envidia*, because he was so jealous of *Papá* Tavo and all of his hard-working children and his house-painting business. No one is really sure why *Papá* Tavo got sick. All we know is that it was never supposed to be like that.

Now, I got near the bed and Pop said, *"Mira, 'Apá: Cirilo."*

Papá Tavo looked at me without any kind of understanding of who I was.

"Es mi hijo, Cirilo," Pop yelled. *"Tu nieto."* He didn't seem to understand I was Pop's son or that I was his grandson. He just stared at the ceiling with his mouth open.

I reached out to shake his hand, and he didn't move at all. I took his hand anyway. It was bigger than mine and cold. *Sus manos.* These hands that had hung drywall and painted houses. These hands that fixed the pickup that I drove, and had rubbed Vicks on my chest when I was a little kid and sick. These hands that had shuffled dominoes.

Just then, *Tío* Gonzalo, *Tía* Victoria, and Little Gonzalo walked into the room.

Pop and *Tío* Gonzalo barely gave each other *saludos*, just a little lifting of the eyebrows and that was it. Pop pretended to wipe some spit away from *Papá* Tavo's face. *Tío* Gonzalo was still mad at Pop for the way he was acting with *'Buelita*. I didn't blame him, even though brothers were not supposed to act this way.

Tía Victoria said, *"¿Y cómo están todos?"* As if no one was mad.

"We're good. Busy with everything, you know how it is."

She said, "*Ay*, tell me about it,"

You could feel things change between Pop and *Tío* Gonzalo. She told me, "Long time no see, stranger," and we laughed. It was great how women could do this, make things better just by being there.

Tío told Little Gonzalo to go give *Papá* Tavo his *saludo*. "*Saludale, mi'jo*. Go say hi to your grandfather."

Little Gonzalo reached forward and picked up *Papá* Tavo's hand, not scared like my other little cousins were, not scared like Sef who would act bored to try and hide it, and not even walk into *Papá* Tavo's room. *Tía* Victoria was a home health nurse and she sometimes took Little Gonzalo on her visits because the old people liked him. He was never scared of them like most kids so they would always ask *Tía* Victoria about him. I didn't know if he wasn't scared because he had seen so many old people sick in their beds or because that was just the way he was. Little Gonzalo turned *Papá* Tavo's hand over and over, and looked at all the wrinkles, the bruised veins and the brown liver spots. He said, "*'Buelito*, what's all this?"

We all kind of laughed at how Little Gonzalo didn't care what he said, at how he was the only one who talked to *Papá* Tavo that way. I thought all that about him being a *chillón* mama's boy didn't matter because Little Gonzalo was brave in his own way, in a way none of the rest of us were or ever would be.

It was quiet and none of us knew what to say. Then, after a little while, *Papá* Tavo looked down at Little Gonzalo and he actually smiled. I couldn't understand him real good because whenever he did talk it sounded like he was half-asleep, like he had glass marbles in his mouth or something. He said, "*Esto, mi nieto, es un mapa donde he estado, donde he vivido.*"

I looked down at his hands, and I knew what he meant about his hands being a map of where he had been and where he had lived. On his hands, I could read where *Papá* Tavo had been: the large spots were places he had stayed, the smaller ones the places he had visited, every wrinkle a dusty *sendero* he had taken to get him here across the river, every vein a street he had used to get him to work, the clear spaces in between where he had never been and never would go. I turned my own hands over and held them out. The map was mostly clear with large open spaces I would claim for the Izquierdos, clear with undiscovered trails and roads I would map out for *Papá* Tavo. Along the way, I would meet others and tell them about what I had seen and what I knew.

Oscar and the Giant
by David Bowles

TOWARD THE END OF MY JUNIOR YEAR, THINGS GOT really bad. I mean, it was tough enough living in the projects, in one of the Section-8 apartments across the street from the Pharr Community Center, standing in for an absent dad with my little brother, Fernando. Mom was working two jobs, my girlfriend had dumped me because I didn't have money to take her out, and the cheap guitar my cousin gave me had a warped neck. I thought life sucked about as bad as it could.

But then I went and insulted Bernard.

I was standing with Javier Vásquez and Luis Serrano, my two best friends, on the steps to the auditorium at PSJA High School one morning, the bus having dropped us off at an ungodly hour, like usual. A random assortment of *cholos*, preps, and nerds made fun of my long hair and torn jeans as they passed. Like usual. I was wearing these turquoise Converse high-tops that my mom had saved up to buy me, and that really got them going.

"*Freak!*" one of them jeered. "*¡Pinche mariposón!*" said another. He couldn't do better than to call me queer. Others were a little more creative with their insults. I normally just brushed this stupidity off, but that morning...I don't know. Maybe because Diana had broken up with me, I just wasn't in the mood to be stepped on anymore. So when Bernard Ayala came trouncing up the steps and muttered, "Out of the way, girlfriend," I wasn't thinking anything except enough was enough, so I snapped and yelled at the effeminate freshman, "Hey, Bernard!"

He turned around, an eyebrow arched. "Yes, O Freaky One?"

"Dude, it's okay to be gay and all, but do you have to be such a drama queen? It's really obnoxious."

Javi and Luis looked at me like I had lost my mind.

Bernard's eyes narrowed. "Oh, Oscar Garza. You idiot."

And then he stormed off, flouncing dramatically. Big surprise.

"Oscar," Luis muttered, "you just insulted Simón Ayala's little brother, man."

I swallowed hard because my own stupidity had just caught up with me. Simón Ayala was the head of the Tri-City Bombers, the notorious street gang that managed petty crime in the Pharr-San Juan-Alamo area. He was in prison, but all the little wannabes at PSJA High School did his bidding, obeying whatever commands he sent through his lieutenants.

"I know." My voice trembled. *"Pero me vale."* I tried to sound tough. But truth was, I knew I'd just stepped into some trouble I probably couldn't handle.

THE FOLLOWING DAY, THERE WERE NO MORE INSULTS, WHICH was odd because all night long I was dreading the sure tongue-lashing to come. Instead, I was tripped, repeatedly, in the hallways. After that, I got my head slammed into a locker, twice. My Converse were stolen during P.E., and I had to borrow Javi's extra shoes, a pair of Payless canvas slip-ons. Damián and Elías, a couple of 19-year-old sophomores, started following me everywhere. They had a host of new nicknames for me, including my favorite, *güero cacahuatero.* I stepped out of class, and there they'd be, right behind me.

"¿Qué onda, güerito?" Damián would say. "Got any clever remarks today, *ese?"*

"Yeah." Elías was a big brute who could only repeat his buddy's words. "What up, *ese?* We want to hear your clever remarks."

I knew better than to address them. The rest of the day they shoved me from behind, or tripped me, or slammed me into a locker, but I kept my mouth shut. And I *damn* sure didn't go near a bathroom. That would have been suicidal. *Grin and bear it,* I told myself. *You've been through worse.* And I had. My dad had taken off on us when I was fourteen years old, leaving me to be the man of the house, according to my mother. Which meant dropping out of sports in middle school. No swim team. No track. So if this was the worst Simón's lackeys could dish out, it was bearable.

In the coming days, Javi and Luis did what they could to help me. They convinced a lot of the wanksters to back off, that I wasn't worth the trouble. Luis was in JROTC, and he and his military-loving classmates intervened a couple of times, kept me from getting too hurt. But my friends couldn't always be around. We had different classes, and just when the attacks seemed to stop, Damián or Elías appeared out of nowhere to torture me some more. It became clear to me that for the most part I was alone in this. I needed to figure out how to fend for myself.

Not the first time, and probably not the last. If I can just make it through one last six weeks, I told myself. *Summer will start, and I'll be free of them.*

One day, I saw Damián talking to Diana, his arm around her, right beneath the mesquite tree where I had asked her to be my chick. The flunky saw me looking and smiled like a happy predator. I should've let it go.

Instead, I flipped him off. It was a stupid thing to do. The physical attacks had basically stopped by then. But I couldn't control myself. He had crossed a line.

When his face twisted in rage, I knew I had really screwed up. Up to now, the conflict had been about Simón defending his pretty brother. Now it was about Damián's *honor*. I almost skipped the rest of the day, but when I got close to the fence, Officer Limón yelled for me to get my butt back to class. So I did, and the hours dragged on in miserable anticipation.

After school I didn't see either of the goons. Looking back and forth to make sure, I made a beeline to the bus and slumped into my customary seat. Luis was at a JROTC fieldtrip and Javi was home sick, so I was alone today, able to stretch my legs and relax for the ridiculously long bus ride home. As I got comfortable, I glanced at the back of the bus.

There they sat. Damián with a psychopathic grin on his face, Luis almost drooling in his Neanderthal idiocy. I quickly looked away, but I could feel their eyes on me during the whole roundabout journey, down 281 to Las Milpas, then a right on Dicker, stopping what seemed every ten feet to drop someone off, then another right to head north on Jackson. *It figures they'd wait until Javi and Luis weren't around*, I kept thinking. *Life's like that. When the crap starts flying, you're on your own.* Finally the bus turned onto Kelly and hissed to a stop not far from the housing complex where I lived. We were the last ones on the bus. I got off and started walking as fast as I could without flat-out running. Even cowardly rockers have their pride.

"Where you going?" a voice crooned just over my shoulder, and one of the punks shoved on my books, sending them flying. I let them fall, beginning to run in earnest now. *Forget pride*, I thought. *I don't want the crap beat out of me!*

My feet pounded the asphalt of our parking lot. I made it to the stairs that led up to the second-floor apartment and dashed up to the landing, where I turned around and saw them looking up at me, laughing. I felt trapped in a pattern that kept repeating itself: abandoned, I tried to face some horrible circumstance only to find my will to resist faltering. *Where is my father?* I wanted to scream. *Where are my friends? Where is God? Am I really expected to stand alone, again, and take a beating?* All the crap that had happened to me over the past four years, all the rage I had pushed down deep in order to survive…all of it came bubbling to the surface, squeezing my chest and making my vision go hazy. The flunkies' jeers were like goads to a bull. Without thinking, I struck out. I wanted to erase those smiles from their faces *so badly*.

I was outmatched physically, so I opened up my big, smart mouth and let them have it. *"Ah, qué pobres mensos, los dos.* You guys think you're so freaking bad, pushing me around at school, chasing me down, knocking my books out of my hands…it's pathetic. *Son unos pinches perdedores.* You're what…19? And still sophomores? Why do you even bother? Yeah, maybe I live in the *barrio* and stuff, but do you really think I'm going to stay here? Have you seen my GPA? My ACT scores? I've got a life ahead of me. I'll go to college, get a good job, marry a beautiful girl. My life is going to be freaking *awesome. ¿Pero ustedes?* What are you going to do, huh? Keep collecting welfare? Knock up some desperate fourteen-year-old? Get a job digging ditches?" My hands were trembling, my mouth dry, my heart pounding. I felt dirty, but I went on. "You realize, right, that no one would miss you if you disappeared today? That your lives don't make a freaking *difference* to anything or anyone? Why don't you just kill yourselves now, get it over with? It's like you don't even exist."

Something horrible happened to Damián's face, as if every blood vessel in his forehead and temples was about to burst. Then he started coming up the stairs, crouched like a hungry predator. Luis circled around and came up the other stairwell, the two of them converging on the landing. I thought about heading to the apartment, but if Fernando wasn't there, I'd have to fish my key out of my pocket, and there just wasn't enough time. So I swung over the railing and dropped to the asphalt, backing away. They came back down, and Damián pulled a switchblade from his pocket.

"*Pinche loco fregado,*" he spat. "Nobody talks to me like that."

I spun and ran like I had never done in my life, sprinting down Kelly and across the crazy late-afternoon traffic on Jackson. I risked a glance over my shoulder, but they were coming like hellhounds, closer and closer. I crossed a weedy field, heading toward the construction site near the expressway. *Got to find something to defend myself with*, I vaguely thought. My lungs were burning, and the muscles in my legs screamed at me to stop. Slipping under the perfunctory fence they'd put up, ignoring the danger signs, I jogged past back-hoes and cranes, scurried over piles of lumber, edged along mountains of dirt and cement block.

And then the ground went out from beneath me, and I fell.

I rolled over in the dust, trying to get my wind back. I had stepped too close to the excavations they'd made for the foundation of whatever building was going up at the site. As I got to my knees, looking around at the five-foot walls that surrounded the huge space, I noticed a strange outline in the dirt before me. It seemed as if I was crouching on the chest of some enormous buried statue. Forgetting about my pursuers, I leaned forward and brushed red dust from what looked like its face: a broad forehead, a nose the size of my fist, a jutting chin.

When I drew my hand away, *its eyes opened*.

Startled, I scrabbled backward, moving away as quickly as I could in a crab-like scuttle. As my back hit the wall of dirt behind me, Elías and Damián leapt into the pit, chests heaving. They moved in. I was cornered.

"*Ahora vas a ver.*" Damián gestured with his knife. "See if you still think you're all that with a couple holes in your chest, *güey.*"

There was movement behind him: two massive hands, breaking free of the clay, pressing down on the packed earth, pushing a gigantic torso away from the ground.

"Dude," I said, pointing over Damián's shoulder, "you should probably look behind you."

"I look stupid to you?" Damián turned to Elías. "*Agárrame a este pinche vato.*"

The figure emerging from the dirt was now sitting, the top of his head extending about a foot above that of Elías. Sand drained in rivulets down the giant's bare chest. His eyes narrowed as he focused on the scene in front of him.

Elías yanked me to my feet. I was too stunned to even attempt to pull away. Damián's blade flashed in the afternoon light.

"Think you got a life ahead of you, *ese*? Think again. *A ver quién te extraña a ti, méndigo.*"

He swung the knife toward me, but his arm was suddenly jerked back. The giant had reached out and grabbed him, yanking him away from me. With a rumbling grunt, the enormous creature stood, rocks tumbling from what appeared to be leather leggings, stitched from a half-dozen different species of animal. Elías's hands slipped away from my shoulders. His jaw was wide open.

"What the...?" he managed to mutter. Damián struggled in the giant's grasp, looking like a rag doll or something. With his left hand, the strange being scooped up Elías, too, who began to make sobbing noises. After regarding them both for a few seconds, the giant set them on the edge of the excavation.

"*Corred,*" he growled as he released them, and, man, did they run! I'm betting they didn't stop until they reached their homes in San Juan.

The giant then turned and looked down at me. He stood easily nine feet tall, pure brute muscle like carved granite, but his orange eyes were kind beneath a shock of white hair.

"Thank you," I croaked.

"You are welcome." His voice thrummed through the hard-packed earth like the best subwoofer in the Valley. "I could not permit them to attack. You are unarmed."

"You...you speak English."

"I am a *tlacahueyac*. A giant of the First Sun. The Feathered Lord gave my people the gift of languages when the world was young. I am able to converse with all thinking creatures."

The enormity of what was happening began to sink in. *There is a freaking* giant *standing in front of me!* My knees wobbled a bit.

"How...how long have you been buried in the ground? How can you still be alive? I'm going crazy, right? Those losers knifed me, and I'm hallucinating as I bleed out."

The giant gave a soft, soothing laugh at my sudden panic. "No, human, you are not seeing visions. Nor have you been wounded. Let us begin again. My true name is beyond your ability to pronounce, but other humans once called me *Olontetl*."

He paused. I realized he was waiting for me to introduce myself. "Oh, I'm Oscar. Oscar Garza."

"Well met, Oscar. I am pleased you awakened me, if only to ward you from those fools. But I see my slumber has been long and humans are no longer accustomed to the sight of giants. If you will sit and rest for a time, I will briefly tell you my tale."

I slumped to the ground. He knelt and eased his bulk lower.

"In the First Age of the world, the Feathered Lord, creator and father, formed the white-haired giants. Sturdy as boulders, we went about the earth, taming its wildness and building wondrous works to glorify our maker. But the Lord of Chaos despised our fealty to his younger brother, and so he tempted many giants, transforming them into monstrous jaguars and setting them against their kin.

"It was a dark, dark time. My own father was turned, and he killed most of my family. I escaped with my brother, and we hid in the depths of the mountains for many years. When we emerged, we found our world destroyed; the strongest among us had wielded frightening, apocalyptic magic to defeat the jaguars, but they laid the earth to waste in the process.

"Only twelve of us remained. My brother and I. Ten others. The Feathered Lord drew us to his side and gave us a new commission: to defend his children against destruction. We would sleep for millennia, he told us, but when chaos rose again, we would be awakened.

"And so we passed the ages. I saw the Second ended by the wrath of mighty hurricanes. The Third Age withered, ravaged by storms of angry fire. A flood effaced the world at the end of the Fourth, heralding the time of humans. We strove, we giants, against the devastation, but one by one we fell. Age after age we dwindled. For a time we would stave off the darkness. Order would be restored. We would sleep long centuries. But we always awakened to even greater chaos and despair. With every new era it has become more difficult to fight.

"At the beginning of this Fifth Age, only three of us remained. As humankind spread across the earth, we each went our separate ways, ever watchful. Many times have I been roused to avert chaos. Now you have called me from my dreamless resting, Oscar. You must lead me toward the wrongs that must be righted."

It was too much to take in. The story he told me was unbelievable, but there he knelt: an ancient giant, asking me to command him. I had been weak for so long that my mind boggled at the idea of such power. *The Tri-City Bombers, the drug traffickers, the child-abusers and wife-beaters...all the horrible things I've watched for years now...I can make them stop.*

The sun was low in the sky. Fernando was probably worrying. He might even call mom, and she would take off from work at her second job to come looking for me. I needed to get back. But I couldn't take Olontetl with me.

He was way too big, and I needed to prepare people first. *Javi's uncle has a ranch in Hidalgo*, I remembered. *We could put Olontetl there for a while. Maybe. If I can get Javi to believe. If he doesn't leave me hanging.*

"Okay, I can do that." I stood and got closer to the giant. His breathing reminded me of gusty spring winds, blowing warmth through the mesquite trees, along the crabgrass. "But, Olontetl, you need to stay here another night, okay? I've got to make arrangements, find...allies."

"Of course," he rumbled. "I will rest here until you return. Then we will engage the forces of the Lord of Chaos. Perhaps this time will be the last. Or perhaps I will fall, like my brother did at the end of the Third Age. But we fight, Oscar, because we must. Beauty and order, creation and knowledge...we cannot allow these to be swallowed up by destruction and entropy."

He placed a massive hand lightly on my head, and then he lay back down in the dirt, blending in so completely that I could only make him out by his bright orange eyes and snow-white hair.

"I'll be back in the morning," I promised, and I clambered out of the pit.

WHEN I GOT HOME, FERNANDO WAS STILL AT SPEEDY Espericueta's apartment, watching inappropriate movies on cable. He hadn't even noticed I wasn't home. It was Friday night, but I knew Javi and Luis would be home: they weren't as broke as me, but they didn't have girlfriends or cars, so it's not like they had a lot of choice.

"Dude," I told them both, "meet me outside tomorrow morning at like 8:30. I've got to show you something *you are not going to believe.*" They pestered me for more information, but I knew better than to tell them anything else. They wouldn't believe me without seeing for themselves. No one would.

It was hard going to sleep. I kept imagining Olontetl going up against gangbangers and drug dealers, pimps and *coyotes*. Maybe even hunting down my dead-beat dad and taking care of him as well. *Justice*, I thought over and over. *Finally, justice.*

Somehow, I fell asleep. The alarm went off at 8:15, and I got dressed and brushed my teeth. Mom was pouring herself a cup a coffee. She made a zombie-like movement to say good morning, and I waved distractedly as I rushed out the door.

Javi and Luis were late. I almost screamed in frustration. *Wouldn't you know it? They weren't around yesterday, and they're AWOL again. Just when I really need...*

Someone tapped my shoulder. I spun around, almost raising my fists defensively. My friends were standing there nonchalantly, Javi's eyes bleary with sleep, Luis's face split in a lop-sided grin.

Alright, that's a relief.   But I wouldn't have been surprised if they hadn't shown up at all.   Morons. I sort of nodded at them in greeting.

"So what's this top-secret crap you want to show us?" Javi asked, stifling a yawn.

"Just come on.   It's over at the construction site near the expressway."

I tried to get them to walk faster, but they ambled along casually, making stupid jokes at my expense. As we crossed the field, I heard the beeping sounds of heavy machinery, the barked orders of supervisors directing workers. *Oh, no*, I thought. *Why are they working on Saturday?*

Rushing to the excavation, I felt nausea rising in my gut. Two large cement trucks were pulling away, their rotating mixers visibly empty. As helmeted men yelled at me to stop, I ran to the edge of the pit and dropped to my knees in despair. It had just been filled with concrete, tons and tons of it, gleaming palely in the morning sun.   Tubes jutted like gravestones from the vast, gray expanse.

"He's gone." A sob wracked my aching chest.

Javi and Luis caught up to me.   "What, dude?" Javi demanded.   "What are you freaking out about?"

"He's gone," I repeated.   "And now I've got to face it all alone."

Luis knelt beside me.   "Oscar, I don't know what's wrong, but you're not alone, man. *Somos cuates, ¿que no?* Me and Javi, we got your back, brother. We'll get those punks to back off, somehow. Now, come on, man. You're scaring me."

I stood and tried to casually wipe the tears from my cheeks. Ashamed of my doubts, I looked at them both with different eyes: the crazy military brat whose dad died in some foreign land, the scrawny migrant kid who lived half the year in Washington. I thought of my own self, a poor nobody with a brain but not much else. We weren't giants, the three of us. We probably didn't stand a chance against the darkness that assailed us.

But we would keep fighting.

igs photos 2013

The Noise Expert
by Jan Seale

TOLD MY HOUSE MOTHER THAT FIRST DAY I'M NOT WEAR-
ing my sweater to work at the airport. I didn't tell her
that a sweater does not make a noise worth a flip. I only
said, I'm wearing my nylon jacket or nothing. (It goes
Shee! Shee! under my arms.)

That was just the beginning of the trouble I had
here at Eats-on-the-Run, before I got things fixed about me
and loud. Some people never will understand, but no matter.
As long as Lonny and Imogene do. How I can't see my hands
and feet without loud. How when it's quiet around me I start
to fade like paints gone watery, soaking into the paper. How
noise is like medicine and mother and daddy to me.

The only one who halfway knew in the beginning was
Imogene. Her face is so shiny it looks on fire. First day, I said
to her, "Please, Imogene, I don't like soft tacos. Just the ones
that go Crack! I want four."

"Richy boy, you a sassy thing," Imogene said. "I gonna
make you tacos when you bite 'em they 'splodes like hand
gernades."

And every morning after that, when I opened the kitchen door, Imogene called out, "Here come Mr. Clatterty-bang!"

She was close. But it seemed like almost everybody else didn't care if I lived or died. "DBQ at DFW." Death By Quiet at the Dallas-Ft. Worth Airport. If I ever make a movie, that's what I'll call it. (I say DFW fast so people think I'm a pilot.)

IT ALL STARTED WHEN THEY CHANGED OVER FROM REAL TO FAKE dishes. My first job here at Eats-on-the-Run was supervisor of washing real dishes and silverware. I drew those plates off the line—slop to the right, paper to the left—then Crash! like two police cars on television down into the pre-rinse.

Imogene would kind of compliment me on it. She'd say, "Richy, you bustin' them suds like a giant o' sorts." Then I would hold my breath and make my chest hard.

I loved it best when a lot of dishes came through at once. They made more noise together. I knew people could see me. I knew I was standing there. My hands and feet showed up just fine.

And mornings, because more cups and saucers. The cups sounded Puck! like they swallowed their own selves when they hit the water.

After the pre-rinse, I got to load the dishes in the dishwasher. Clunk! and Phum! It was great.

Silverware? Wires, bells, slinky toys. When I dumped the soak bucket in the sink, everybody in the kitchen looked around. Once the dishwasher was full, I was to tell Imogene and she'd come turn it on for me. The water started up with a roar and that's when I'd lean against the machine and re-tie my shoes. When I could feel the noise, I was Okay Operational.

Then came the day everything changed and I had to work hard to keep myself from disappearing.

I WENT IN THAT DAY AS USUAL AND I WASHED DISHES UNTIL after Flight 117 came through. (Those passengers are all hungry by the time they get to us. Eats-on-the-Run is not like your ordinary cafe—we got our busy times according to the airplanes on our concourse—we're special.)

By then it was afternoon and Mr. Perkins, my super who is not even as old as I am but who talked to the people at the Home about me working here, came in and said, "Richy, guess what? This is your last load of dishes."

I dried my hands quick on my apron and put them in my pockets. After I'd done a load, I'd keep my hands in my pockets as long as they'd let me because my fingers looked like soft pickles. They scared me 'til they got hard again.

I started to cry, thinking they weren't going to let me work at Eats anymore. Mr. Perkins said, "Wait, Richy! All I meant was, we're going to plastic."

If I had of known how hard it was to make noise with plastic, I would have kept on crying.

Now they put me out front cleaning tables and stuff. The first few days I missed the sounds of the dishes so much I thought about quitting, but what would I say: "I'm quitting because no one can see me anymore"? I whistled a little bit, but no one paid much attention to me. I had to think up new ways to make loud.

This is what I figured out: When I went to clean off a table, I folded the styrene soup bowl in half and crammed it in the small styrofoam coffee cup, then twisted it—
so I got a Screech! Then poked that upside down into the jumbo styrofoam. If I caught the two cups just right, they sounded Pow! like boxers.

Next I took the plastic silverware (boy, is that name a laugh!) and folded it in a napkin and broke it. At first I just popped it with my bare hands but the plastic cut me up and Mr. Perkins said if I thought I should break it, be sure to roll it in a napkin first.

When I got through clearing the table, I was supposed to check the booth seats too. Then's when I found a new noise. If I saw a crumb or anything at all, I let fly with my rag, just hit that seat over and over until the thing bounced off. It felt good to be giving something a spanking. The vinyl was better than a behind for hitting.

Sometimes, especially if it was on the long seat by the divider, I'd pop the rag right next to a lady and she'd jump a mile. I guess she thought I was coming at her with that rag.

"It's okay, lady," I'd say. "I have to clean the seats." This way I got to say something to the customers.

And every now and then through the day I managed a bunch of noise with the garbage sacks for the pitch-in. The sacks are folded up in a tight square, so I shook them out—four, five, six times if Mr. Perkins wasn't around—before I put my arms inside and took the corners clean to the bottom of the tub. It got to where everybody in the whole place would be looking at me when I finished.

So, between me screeching the styrofoam, popping the seat with my rag, and shaking the pitch-in sack, I was hanging on. I adapted, as my counselor at the Home says to do. And besides, I still got to wash the pots and pans in the afternoon.

That is, until Lonny came, from another Home, and Mr. Perkins said for him to take over my job of washing up the pots and pans. I hated Lonny right off. They should let you keep your first noises.

I don't care if I *did* get good with the fake dishes, I still loved my pots and pans. There was this one lid that sounded like a cymbal from Lawrence Welk if I hit it with a spoon just right. I always asked Imogene, "Did you use my lid today? I need to fix my head with it."

"Richy, you crazy!" she'd say. I liked her. She treated me great. I never heard her tell Lonny he was crazy or anything like that.

So I was really mad at Lonny in the beginning. I didn't say a word to him, not even hello, when he came in, mornings. He'd say, "Hi, Richy," but I pretended I didn't hear.

Then we all found out Lonny couldn't remember anything. Sometimes he left his rag on the table. Or his spray bottle right in the middle of a table along with the ketchup and napkins. And his van driver had to come in and get him in the afternoons because he couldn't remember when to stop work.

After about a week, there Lonny is, standing beside me at the window one morning when I am on my break watching Flight 37 take off. Lonny's head is long and his chest is kind of caved in. He looks soft all over.

We are both standing there looking out, pretending we don't see the other one. I always keep my hands on the glass; I like to feel the rattle when a plane takes off. So when a 747 in the next gate turned around and started taxiing out to the runway, Lonny says, "You like noise, don't you?" Just like that.

I keep looking out the window and try not to grin. "How'd you know?"

"I been watching you," Lonny says.

We walked back together, but I told myself he came along with me because he didn't know when he was supposed to go back. From then on, when it was time for my break, I went back to the kitchen and told everybody, "I'm going on my break now. I'll be over at Gate 6."

"Okay, honey," Imogene would say. "We come find you if we get a rush on."

And after I'd walk over there and be studying the runways real hard, I'd feel a person beside me and it would be Lonny.

I guess we looked funny, standing there in our white aprons and hats, both of us with our hands flat up against the glass waiting for Flight 37 to take off for London.

Finally one day Lonny said, "That airplane sound scares me to death."

I looked at him. He was staring straight out at the planes. "Then why do you come to the noise?" I asked him.

"Because I'd rather be with you and your noises than myself," he said.

After that, I began helping Lonny remember more. Before, Mr. Perkins had had to tell Lonny a bunch of times about leaving his wipe-up rag on a table. Lonny would be back in the kitchen asking for another rag and Mr. Perkins would say, "Go look for your rag, Lonny. I bet it's on a table." Sometimes Lonny's eyes got red around the rims.

Now I would watch and when Lonny started to leave his rag on the table, I would bust out singing a Kenny Rogers song. It wasn't very long until Lonny caught on.

But pretty soon my own troubles started up again. One of our customers with a fur coat complained about me. Here's how it happened.

When I see something soft, I have to make more noise than ever. Otherwise, the soft will suck up my ordinary sounds and there I'll go, getting dimmer and dimmer.

So when this lady came in on an afternoon flight and threw her coat on the long vinyl seat, I made my way over there as soon as I could and started beating the seat beside it with my rag.

She already had a cigarette and coffee and was talking to her daughter. The first hit, she jumped sky high.

"Jesus! What is wrong with you?" she said, real loud, and the loud in her voice was nice but the words weren't. Her hair was pricked up like Woody Woodpecker's in front.

Most people jump and look at me if I beat the seat close to them but they don't say anything. This time I didn't know what to say back. "I like the loud, is all."

"What kind of an answer is that?" she asked her daughter. Then she got right up and went to Mr. Perkins and said I had tried to hit her with my rag. She was traveling from one hospital to another with a nervous disorder and I was the straw that broke the camel's back. Besides all that, she had a friend who knew a person on the airport board.

Mr. Perkins told her he was real sorry and he'd take care of it. He called me to go help Lonny with the pots and pans. At quitting time Mr. Perkins told me to wait to clean the long side seat until there was nobody sitting on it. That's all.

So the next day, I missed the *Pop! Pop!* of the seat because there was somebody on it practically all day. A kid ate a croissant all over it and Mr. Perkins sent Lonny to wipe up the crumbs. Lonny didn't even forget his rag. It all made my stomach hurt.

The next morning Mr. Perkins gave Lonny my job of changing the plastic garbage sacks. Lonny couldn't make a sound worth a dime with them. You got to hold on to the top tight and punch your hands up and out in front of you until the sack comes down like a parachute. I showed Lonny, but he only did little jerks down the front of himself until the sack opened. He was too soft.

The next day Mr. Perkins brought a pink plastic tub to my cart and told me not to break the forks and spoons, not even rolled in a napkin—just put them all together in a heap. And to stack in separate stacks the soup bowls, the cheesecake saucers, the divided plates. To put the small, medium, large drink cups all by themselves. He had caught on to me.

The day after that I couldn't get out of bed. I told my house father I had a sore throat. I lay in bed all that day, and the next and the next. The medicine they gave me made me feel funny.

The fourth morning my house father came in. "Richy," he says, "I talked to Mr. Perkins yesterday. I think your sore throat is better."

"Nobody cares about me anymore," I say. "I might as well not be there, what with Mr. Perkin's new rules."

"Go to work today, Richy," my house father says. "You remember what adapting means, don't you?"

Lonny was waiting for me at the service entrance. "Hi, Richy," he said. I didn't look at him. I went on in. I rattled my jacket hanging it up and got my apron and hat. Lonny was right there beside me.

"We fixed it," he said.

"Fixed what?" I said.

"Fixed your loud," he said. He took a little radio out of his pocket.

Imogene turned down her grill and came over. She reached for her purse on the shelf and brought out a package. It was wrapped in plastic and she handed it to Lonny, but he was too soft to open it. I took it from him and broke out the hard plastic window with a good Snap! It was headphones and Lonny took them and plugged them in to the radio. Then he put the headphones on me and handed me the radio.

The music went straight to the middle of my brains. Drums up behind my nose. Guitars taking off on my tongue.

Imogene wiped her face on her apron and started grinning. I could see her lips moving. "Imogene to Richy...over!"

"I read you, Imogene." I must have said it real loud. Everyone in the kitchen looked around. Lonny had put a piece of tape over the volume button so it wouldn't go soft.

"Can you see me?" I asked them.

"Yes, but you've got to keep your radio on," Lonny said.

"And eat a lot of them loud tacos," Imogene said.

Then we all went back to work.

The Naked Woman on Poplar Street
by Diane Gonzales Bertrand

NO ONE ON THE SALVADOR HIGH SCHOOL CROSS country team believed Camo Salinas when he said he saw a half-naked woman on Poplar Street.

"You're nuts," Lucas Vera told him. "You were probably thinking about some woman to take your mind off the burn, and you started hallucinating, man."

"I'm telling you, I saw her—she had a robe on, but it was down around her waist. She was showing off her *sandías*, Lucas—big ones, too." Camo wiped the sweat off his face and smeared it across the top of his shirt. "I'm telling you, Joe, there's a naked woman waiting for us on Poplar Street."

"Okay, man." Joe Morales pressed his locker closed and turned around. "After we change, we'll get back in your truck and look for her."

The three guys had been friends since they got cut from the freshmen football team last year. The track coach took them in, but they had no idea that all track athletes had to also run cross country in the fall. Camo, Lucas, and Joe were lousy distance runners, but with so few members, no one got cut from the team. Finding a naked woman on the running route could give the three of them bragging rights, and earn a little respect from the seniors who had named them *Stumblers* from the very first practice.

So they showered and hauled it out to Camo's '99 Ford pick-up in record speed. And the search began.

Camo had to drive a few miles before he got to the corner of Poplar Street and Evergreen that was part of their run every afternoon. By now, traffic was thick with rush hour and each boy in the truck cruising slowly down Poplar felt a thickness growing in his gut. Camo slowed down to follow the street where they had run two hours before, but the neighborhood was different with kids riding bikes, old men watering the grass, and a few men sharing beers and stories at work trucks parked in their driveways.

"Which house was it?" Lucas asked. He rode shotgun. As soon as they turned the corner, he rolled down the window, slung his arm out and gave each house an avid stare. "Do you remember?"

"Not sure," Camo answered. He cursed under his breath. "One minute I slow down and I'm rolling a cramp out of my neck, and boom—there she is, right behind a screen door, showing me her stuff."

Joe, who was squeezed between them in the front cab, shifted his knees against the dashboard. "So did you stop and talk to her, man?"

"Naw, I just kept running—I was already a block behind the rest of the team, and Coach's already on my case for being a slacker, so I took off."

The guys drove up and down Poplar Street for twenty minutes, but no one spotted anyone naked anywhere.

The next day after school the sophomores agreed to run as a pack, but even with everyone looking, nobody spotted the woman. They broke into their own patterns as they ran around Elm Street Ditch, especially when it started raining, and no one cared about anything but getting back to the gym and out of cold clothes. Before they made the second loop through Poplar Street, Camo dropped back with a painful stitch under his ribs and fell behind. He jogged in place a few moments, rubbing his ribs. He took a deep cleansing breath and glanced at a nearby house.

There she stood—only this time, there was no robe. He could see a naked woman as if she was covered by a gray mist—but it was really only a dirty screen.

Camo's mouth dropped open in a gasp that almost choked him. The rain hit his tongue, making him gag on saliva, shock, and wow. He started to yell out at Lucas and Joe at the end of the block, but a rumble of thunder made him realize he needed to get off the street or lightning could fry him like a chicken leg.

By the time he ran and caught up to the others, they were all running in heavy, cold rain.

Once inside the locker room Camo exclaimed, "I saw her again."

Lucas whipped a towel in his direction. "Camo, how stupid do you think we are?"

But Joe did a quick turn. "You saw the woman again? Naked?"

"Yeah, this time there was no robe. She stood behind a dirty screen. I could tell she had long hair," Camo told them.

Lucas frowned. "I think lightning cracked your brain."

"I swear! On the sacred head of my dead *abuelo*!" Camo's fingers crossed over his heart for dramatic effect. "I'm telling the truth about a naked woman on Poplar Street."

Once again the sophomores piled into Camo's truck and drove back to Poplar. This time, Camo swore he could recognize the house by its screen door. Who would have guessed that every house on Poplar Street had dirty screen doors?

THE FOLLOWING DAY AS PRACTICE STARTED, THE THREE GUYS promised to work together to spot the woman. They let the rest of the team get a couple of blocks ahead and then the three of them slowed down, despite the chewing out they faced from Coach for lousy times.

Once they reached Poplar Street, Lucas said, "Camo, you go first, since you've seen her before. And if you don't see her, maybe one of us will get lucky!"

Camo ran solo down Poplar Street hoping to spot her. He didn't, so he jogged in place at the corner and motioned Joe to run down next.

Once Joe reached him, Camo asked, "Did you see her?"

"Don't you think I would have stopped and asked her name, idiot? Why would I run to you when I could stare at her?" Joe's anger was easy to ignore. Of all of them, Joe was always the horniest.

Both guys gestured to Lucas to run towards them, but no woman appeared. Each of them took a turn running back and forth on the street until they knew they needed to run to the ditch before the upperclassmen figured out the sophomores never ran the full length of the trail Coach had set up for training.

But Coach was waiting outside the gym for the Stumblers. "The past two days you three have been coming back long after everyone else. What's up?"

Joe mumbled something about cramps, Lucas blamed it on his dad refusing to buy him new shoes. Camo shrugged and played dumb. Coach didn't buy it.

"You stay up with the team, or there'll be hell to pay," he told them and walked towards the coaches' office, munching on a bag of *chicharrones*.

Lucas and Joe stared hard at Camo. He decided to play dumb a while longer.

They saw nothing the next two weeks, so Camo decided it was some optical illusion or maybe just a head dream from pushing himself to run harder. The others eventually forgot about it too. The three sophomores were still at the end of the pack in running the route, but their times improved a little, so at least Coach left them alone.

ON A WEDNESDAY, A WEEK OR SO AFTER GRADES CAME OUT AND the team lost two of the best runners to no-pass no-play, Camo ran ahead of his two friends down Poplar Street. He found a comfortable stride, when he glanced at a faded wooden house with a chunky front porch, and saw the woman once more.

He had finally found the house again. Hard as it was, he took his eyes off the woman for just an instant to look at the house number above the door. He mouthed the numbers 7-2-7. Now he had proof for the guys, and then the three of them would be the envy of the track team. The older runners would be so jealous.

7-2-7.

7-2-7.

Camo played it cool, and ran around a small circle on the front sidewalk, until he slowed to a jog and ran back to meet Lucas and Joe puffing up the road. He merely said,

"There she is." He jogged a circle around them, and then said, "7-2-7."

Camo repeated the numbers again and again until Lucas and Joe started chanting with him. And like a pack of horny dogs, they ran toward the house, slowing down, jogging in place, staring at the woman on the porch.

They saw big breasts, the fleshy middle, and her bare legs from under the door slat covering her most private parts. Sweat rolled down their backs, cooling their sizzling skin. Each boy stared passionately at the wisps of long hair, hanging over her bare shoulders. A curtain of shadows from the afternoon sun was keeping her face hidden, but they still got an eyeful of skin and dark curves.

Slowly she stepped from behind the door. The boys kept jogging in place, their legs heavy and throbbing. Who would be the first to speak?

Then she opened her brown arms wide to the boys. A second later, every lustful thought shattered hard in grim reality: an old woman's face! An old woman's body! Like somebody's grandma, and who wanted to see their grandma naked?

The boys stumbled blindly into each other. They raced away from the house, running fast towards the ditch.

TOGETHER THEY DECIDED NOT TO RUN BACK THROUGH POPLAR, but take another route back to the school. They would face Coach's wrath like a team—probably two weeks of 5:00 am runs in addition to the afternoon runs they had every day but Sunday. It felt like a fair penalty after staring at a naked old lady.

They chose silence and punishment—stoic and proud—but really there was no pride in what they knew. And before they reached the gym, they all agreed to tell Coach there were just too many loose dogs on Poplar Street, and he should find the team another practice route for the rest of the season.

POETRY

Relocating Emotions

by Guadalupe García McCall
Piedras Negras, Coahuila, Mexico - Summer 1984

I was suffocating,
fastidiada,
at my wit's end
with my father,
my sisters, my brother.
Perhaps it was the feverish
heat of the brutal sun,
or maybe it was the exhaustion
of sweltering on the porch
listening to the incessant
chirping of the love-sick *chicharras*
that infuriated me most.
Maybe it was the thin
rivulets of sweat crawling
down my dark face draining me
with their painstaking slowness
that drove me insane.

I only knew I hated
the blasted whiteness
of that summer.
Heat engulfed me
as I watched the drops
of my sweat and tears
fall silently
and then evaporate
on the cement
of the front porch
of my father's house.

After much debate
in the hot kitchen of that
oppressive house,
I packed my denim duffel bag.
Two pairs of jeans, two t-shirts,
socks, and underwear.
Enough clothes to last me
all summer
if I scrubbed every day.

In Mexico
mi abuela Nacha gave me
a thin, linen nightgown,
azul celeste, the color
of a cleansing pool.
I slipped into it and lay down to pray.
I prayed for Mami.
I prayed for my sisters
and my brothers too.
I even prayed for my father.
My face was still wet
when I finally fell asleep.

A tinkling, tiny sound,
like cheerful raindrops
bouncing off glass,
dancing on windowsills,
wove itself into my dream
as I awakened to the brightness
of morning sunlight
kissing my eyelids.

I followed the
taunting notes into a sunny
bathroom, where I found
a gleeful leak singing forth
from the spigot of a
standing shower with
cool azure walls.

I turned the metal
handle, washed my legs
with the cold, clear
water gurgling from the faucet and
thought about my frustration,
my anger, my pain,
and asked myself,
"How would the Lord
Handle this?"
Jesus was always
So composed and serene.
How does one gain
Such tranquility,
such harmony?
I prayed for peacefulness
as I let gentle water
puddle around my feet,
and then, as in a dream,
I stepped forth
and walked on it.
Happy.
Content.
Un milagro.

The Troop Leader's Daughter

by Katherine Hoerth

Our sticks held just above the quiet flame,
marshmallows turn from white to golden brown.
I sit around the camp fire with the boys
who talk of guts, and how, while hiking through
the woods they found a pigeon's body torn
to pieces in the brush. I plunge my stick
into the pit, marshmallow turns to coal.
The boys burst into laughter, hush their talk
of blood.

If you were lost, what would you do?
my father asks the troop. They talk of earth,
of footprints, broken twigs and skies like maps.
I clutch my precious lucky rabbit's foot,
dyed red and soft against my sweaty palms.

Which one's the North Star, kid?

                                    He asks, his eyes
on me. I shrug and mumble,

                        Dunno, point
my finger to the milky sky at one
of countless specks. A boy scout grabs my arm
and leads my finger toward the Dipper's tail.

Right there,
                he whispers in my ear, his warm
breath tickling my neck. A June bug lands
atop my knee, drunk on our light.
I shriek, the scout lets go my arm and lifts
the clumsy bug with pinching fingertips.
He hurls it to the flame. I watch it burn.

Girl, how will you find your way back home?

Corazón Bilingüe

by Brenda Nettles Riojas

Sin palabras, and without translation

perhaps I prefer the tangled
tongue I negotiate.

Sometimes in English,
sometimes in Spanish,

*y a veces no tengo las palabras
para lo que pienso,
no puedo expresar para que otros me entiendan.*

I keep silent,	some words
caught	between worlds
lost in the currents	of *el Río Bravo*
we call	the Rio Grande
that connect,	divide.

I open my mouth,	and my words hesitate
pulled	in opposite directions.

¿Como se dice?
How do you say what can't be said
without altering meaning,
without changing the song?

*Las Mañanitas que cantaba el Rey David
no suenan igual*
in King David's tongue.

Always I apologize for the pauses and the lost
in the lacuna. *Dispénse me.*

Even the rhythm changes.

My pace interrupted
I pause,   listen to the heart

it beats to more than one language,
translates all.

El Corazón late en todos lenguajes.

Taquería Love
by Minerva Vásquez

I lied for the first time.
Said I was one place, went somewhere else.

A beat-down might come of this.
Who cares.
Coming anyway.
Sooner for Mami, later for me.

Truth,
I've seen Ethan every day this week,
helping him with a project after school.
Art room. 317.

Except today. He shows up, takes my elbow, whispers *let's go*.

Lie,
I hated not telling the truth.
Lie,
nobody I know saw us.
Lie,
Ethan is just a boy, a crush.
Lie,
I know what to do with boys.

Truth,
he took me to a *taquería* north side of town. *Salsa verde* with lime juice over *tacos de bistek*. Green bowls of *frijoles al la charra*, steaming over tables draped with *manteles* embroidered with Mexican flowers. Drinking *limonada*.

Finding me. Finding him. His shoulder pulling me in. Art in the truest sense with words, smiles, all kinds of happy talk, his eyes on me.

He dropped me off a block away from home, but not without showing me what to do.

Close eyes, wait for lips, his hand on my neck, smell of him engulfing all.

A brisk walk home, holding my body close, savoring goosebumps of 90 degree weather, Valley weather. October cicadas chiming in CAPS LOCK under leaves. My scarves waiting in drawers, anticipating fall. Ready to drown in long embrace.

Heft

by José Antonio Rodríguez

The cafeteria doors give,
everybody runs bow-legged-joy
to the playground—metal bars,
tether-ball post,
the yellow curves on concrete
collaring the basketball hoop.

I skitter to the tree—
tell no one of its canopy
umbrella to the dumpster—
the bark like the teacher's scowl,
the flies tickling my eyelids

like the moment just after
the punch-line. So many ants
mapping trails around my feet only,
the sweet stench of sugar and then,
stoic against the refuse,

boxes and boxes of ice cream bars:
Push-ups, FudgeBombs, Eskimo Pies,
and those red-white-and-blue ones
called Fourth of July's.
I've seen the wrappers before fall

like autumn leaves from others' fingers,
their pockets and pretend purses heavy
with change because these aren't free
like lunch. But I've never tasted one.
These wrappers though hold shape, heft

placid with frost and no sign with a price,
no grown-up with an open palm
waiting for the money that will
make that thing yours.
Later in the classroom, an American flag

growing out of the wall up high
above the solar system, the teacher
asks if any of us touched that ice cream
thrown out when the freezer broke down.
Doesn't want us getting a stomach ache,

says she'll send us to the nurse.
No one speaks, all plum cheeks and eyes
like questions marks, while I think
of how a bee hovered just above
my hairline—clumsy and trivial—

and then landed like a paper airplane
on the edge of that milky sugar
that would become honey.

Maybe my hands craved a reward.
But how could a gold star ever be enough?
What prize for walking away
crippled with desire, heart-worn with want.

The Smell of Crayons

by César de León

The smell of crayons
talks to me
about an afternoon
when I was five
and you were 31
tucked away in our trailer home
while sister slept
in my old brown crib
and father was working late

the kitchen light yellow
on your hands
and on the table
like the flowers that grew
besides the broken driveway
and the ones on your dress
that folded into each other
when you sat next to me
smelling of soap and *Mazeca*
your freckled arms
white against my brown
tapered into hands and fingers
that would one day turn rough
with work, and life, and motherhood
(but that was still unknown)

sitting there beside me
you took a box of crayons out of a brown paper bag
and opening the box you held it to your nose
closed your eyes and smiled
I watched
and when you gave them to me
I smelled them and smiled
the waxy scent melting and mixing
with your motherly perfume
what memory made you smile?
did the smell of crayons talk to you too
of the childhood you had to share with your sisters?
had you been waiting
in forbidden jealousy
for the moment
when you and only you
could open the virginal box?
was there a revelation, a prophecy, a vision
about the house we would draw
together on the flattened paper bag?
the promised house in the promised land?
or did you know at that moment
that every time I would open a box of crayons
I would smell them
and remember
that afternoon.

Winter *en el Valle*

by Octavio Quintanilla

It is a Valluco winter,
slurping on *raspas de leche* and swimming in canals.
Here, I've never seen a daisy die of frostbite,
never seen a sycamore sob icicles
because a cold wind paws its leaves.
Never seen *chachalacas*
postpone their song because of sore throats.
Yet I've seen men huddle around a fire,
battling days without work,
the cold fronts
not even the Valley heat can thaw.

Lucky One
by Octavio Quintanilla

I was one of the lucky ones who worked in the fields
picking peppers and cucumbers kneeling and dragging my body

because I was too tired to bend
too tired to think about my skin rubbing earth
as if wanting to create a fire
my fingers picking like the beaks
of blackbirds at the carcass of vegetables
fingers reading vines blindly
opening leaves to see what's hid within.

After the picking was done we would walk back to the camp
my brother and I wishing we could go back home
      where we belonged

but grandmother said work made us
into "hombres de bien,"
men of good,
and so I was satisfied with eating canned peas and refried beans
and wiping my greasy mouth on a scarf
and feeling warm inside because of all the clothes
I would buy for school
knowing that most of my buddies would be wearing
the same old pants, the same old shirts, the same old shoes
and I would even have enough money to buy a burger and fries
instead of waiting in the free-lunch line
the whole thought was beautiful
because for once I was the hero of my own life.

But at 5:30 a.m. the enormous sound of the alarm clock
would wake us and once again we would stand quietly
eating our reheated tortillas packed with eggs
cooked with the grease of bacon
looking out the frosty window
into the darkness of November mornings
the headlights of cars and tractors twitching like the eyes of owls
the thickness of the morning's dew
soaking our clothes
feeling wet and smooth like a toothless mouth on our fingers
and no one would talk about the cucumbers
or the green peppers that we would pick that day
no one would talk about the hurried lunch
that perhaps we would not finish eating
or about the fact that it was Sunday
or about the sky that seemed overweight with impending rain
not even about the clawing cramps in our legs

everyone was still dreaming.

Devil at the Dance

by Amalia Ortiz

Her *papá* taught her to never look down.
A good dancer engages her partner's gaze
or trustfully rests an ear on a strong shoulder.
So, by the time she finally noticed   the hoof   the claw
tearing up the floor where shiny boots should be,
it was too late.

She was already in love.

Pinta

by Amalia Ortiz

Tía Irma gave Pinta to Gramma when she moved. Off
went Irma with her husband, three kids, and a dog.
But no cat—no Pinta.

Tía Irma called her "Patches," but "Parchess" came out
when Gramma tried to say it. The little cat was *pintada
como un* patchwork quilt. "*¡Gatita Pinta!*" Gramma
renamed her, and Gramma handed her to me.

Pinta is a girl's best friend. We share *chicharrones*—
stuff ourselves with them—until one of us throws up,
(usually Pinta) but that won't stop the two of us from
skipping down the *calle* to the *tortillería* for more.

The Easter before Grampa died, Gramma said fifth grade
means boys will come too soon. Too old for the baskets!
Too old for the candy! Too old for the egg hunts! Besides,
she didn't have time—not with Grampa in the hospital.

But *Tío* Ruperto went behind her back and bought a basket
bigger than any I had ever had before! Gramma was so mad!
But I loved my uncle—more than I loved that beautiful basket
filled with color and flavor. I vowed I would save it forever.

Now two years later, Pinta comes along and I rig my
last Easter basket to a rope, place Pinta safely inside,
climb the tree out back, and hoist my best friend, Pinta,

up the tree with me. Every weekend, we hide up there,
listen to the radio, and wait for people to pass
down the unpaved alley behind my house.

And with Pinta and my last Easter basket it doesn't matter
that Gramma doesn't allow other kids over.

With Pinta and my last Easter basket it doesn't matter
that I am only allowed to play out back alone.

With Pinta and my last Easter basket it doesn't matter
that Gramma thinks about boys more than I do.

That girls in the seventh grade don't climb trees or play
with cats like I do. Girls at school on Monday mornings
will chatter excitedly about boys

boys at skate parties—boys at group bowling dates
boys at outings I am never invited to anymore
because everyone knows Gramma would just say
"No!"

But with Pinta and my last Easter basket
in a niche between three decaying branches
I can sing loudly, bravely

louder than the shouts from beyond the grey
dusty screen door—old angry ideas protesting
girls climbing trees "¡Ya bajate!"

Just a little while longer, please, in the trees
with my last Easter basket and my *gatita*, Pinta.
My beautiful Pinta—my *Tío* Ruperto later sells when
he is supposed to be cat sitting one summer vacation.

I am told a rich lady admired her unusual markings.
(more likely, she was hit by a car) Ruperto shoves
crumpled bills into my hand, but I do not count them
Today *Tío* is Judas, and I will never be Peter.

My brother, Bene, never lets me forget Pinta every
time we eat *tamales*. He likes to see me cry when he
jokes that whoever really bought Pinta made *tamales*
out of her. I force-feed myself *tamales*. Bene meows.

He May Not Make It

by Edward Vidaurre

I'm writing a story
about this *cholo*
who wakes up in the morning
and lights up a cigarette

checks his phone
and grabs a white t-shirt
and a pair of brown dickie pants
first the shirt
the *burro* is unfolded
and the iron is hot enough

his mom is at work
and little brother in school
my *cholo* decided to skip school
and I'm afraid he may not make it

he looks through the
blinds of his apartment
before setting foot outside
—it's cool
no one's creeping

the *tres flores*
trails behind him
keeping his shadow company
as he walks towards the *barrio*
to meet up with his homies
and I'm afraid he won't make it

fatherless child
a *chicano* mess
he commands
a mother's pain

as the distant cries
are just that
—distant
—non existent

he smiles
at the neighborhood
like he's a hero of sorts
with his limp
and I'm afraid he may not make it

the brothers G
are already glossy-eyed
and swerving each time
a breeze blows by
the ink is drying on teardrop's neck
the oldies sound
beautiful this morning
like an anthem of death
and I'm afraid he may not make it

my *cholo*
is trying to make it
to the end of his story
and I'm afraid he may not make it.

Rock, Paper, Scissors

by Diane Gonzales Bertrand

The game girls play.

Hold a word in your hand,
hurl it at a friend.
Shatter the quiet
with spiteful gossip.

Decorative words
wave in the hallway,
Crumble a note and
toss in a gym trash can.

Slicing words
through a paper heart chain,
snips away confidence,
litters the bathroom floor.

Learn how to win.
Know when
to bash,
to cover,
to cut.

Rock breaks scissors
Paper covers rock
Scissors cuts paper

Try again.

Do These Genes Make Me Look Fat?
by Diane Gonzales Bertrand

Marisela stands on the bathroom scale.
Curses the numbers,
stumbles off and grabs
the *chicharrones* bag.
The *primas* call her "big-boned,"
but she blames the Vásquez *mamás*
insisting extra *manteca* in plump *tamales*
means quality love in every bite.
And don't forget *las tías* who bring
arroz y frijoles to every table.
Even the *chisme* among *las comadres*
isn't delicious without *pan dulce y café*.

Marisela supersizes her fries to conceal
her salty face with greasy fingers.
She gives up zippers,
gets cozy with elastic.
She hates who she sees in the mirror,
knows the nasty names boys use for fat girls.
But what girls say about girls
takes another piece of cake.

Nobody teaches girls willpower
like they teach how to use mascara
or the way a tampon works.
New lessons must be taught
among *mujeres* in *la familia*.
Something besides
the best way to keep *flan*
from jiggling off a plate
mired in its own vanilla sweetness.

La Labor: Migrantes del Valle

by Daniel García Ordaz

I woke daily to the sound of my mother's wooden *palote*
gliding over the kitchen counter where she flattened
the hand-kneaded dough to make flour *tortillas*.

Beans and *tortillas*. *Tortillas con* beans. Beans con *frijoles*.
Tacos wrapped in foil paper to keep them warm,
Wrapped in foil to keep away dust, bugs, and hunger.

We dressed in long-sleeved shirts and hats, and raced
the sun through curving forest roads and drove.

Sometimes, *Tío* Rico would stop to fire at a deer
no one else saw from his window. We drove.

We picked tiny cucumbers for pickling—
their thorny fuzz befriending our skin—
in a clumsy squatted waltz in the fog through endless rows
of green and dirt and sun.

We picked asparagus. Cleaned rows between potato plants, radishes.
We picked banana peppers. Packed potatoes. And drove.
Our fingers smelled of dirt and pesticides.
There was no bathroom in the fields.

The day never ended.
All summer was one day and every day was workday.

'*Apá* would dip our sodas in a cold creek.
We worked and couldn't wait for lunch time
at 10 a.m.

Once, with nothing else to eat in sight,
Nena and I devoured saltine crackers dipped in chocolate frosting.
I was eight.

We'd get back to camp and eat and shower and sleep and begin again.

Sometimes George would catch frogs at the canal before dinner.
Sometimes Arturo would run with Licha from Edinburg,
who was in cross country and had nice legs.

The few Sundays when we didn't work all day we played baseball.
Mom hit a homerun.
Dad played cards until two in the morning.
Marco was his good-luck charm.
Tío Rico danced with a goat on his birthday
and then cooked it.

Minnesota. Wisconsin. Arkansas. Texas.

I hated interstate truck stops
with lights like a surgeon's lamp
that startled us awake.
I feared the spaghetti crisscross highways,
the tall overpasses of the big cities.

One year, on our way home, our station wagon burned.
The engine overheated. The grass caught fire.
Mom saved a blanket she was knitting.
The ball of yarn rolled out of the car, aflame.
My mother prayed about it.
My father wrote a song.
Tío Rico cursed.
We cried.
Max's fishing rods melted to the car.
Half of what we'd earned burned
with that avocado green station wagon.
We moved on.

We were split up and got a ride to the next migrant camp from strangers.
A black trucker dropped off three of us in Hope.
I don't remember how we got home to Texas.

Back home, every season had its crop
Every Saturday its early start.
We picked onions and onions and onions and
cantaloupes and tomatoes and oranges and grapefruits and
onions.

When the teacher asked me to write about where we had gone
during our summer vacation
I always said the same thing:

Nowhere.

when a story is an heirloom

by Priscilla Celina Suárez

their stories are secrets
scented like a river of lavender water
tell-telling a map of where
        they have been
and flowering as a bouquet
of sequences
now settled in my memory,
        parting me into two—
        that which I know is me
        and that which I figure
        becomes a history of me,
a trace, a bloodline, an inheritance,
an atlas
of the worlds before me
and the paths we as an entity
have already taken.

their stories are to be buried
but never hidden
away in the grating lumber chest
my grandparents
brought home from Reynosa. not every moment
has to be so hard
on us
        when the distance
        we travelled
is never far enough
to hide and cry
for fear of belonging…too much to too many.

their stories are rather the worst kind
insisting they have a chance
to exist and re-exist
as they travel

from one ear out one mouth and into another ear.
so they become
a rather fragile
heirloom needing constant care
and renovations
            from the passing and re-enacting
an aunt, a cousin, a son, a nephew
bring to light
with the recollection another story
has triggered.

their stories are like a trance
we as offspring cannot escape,
whether because we respect our elders
when they tell us a boring chronicle
of childhoods spent out in the *labores*
            or because we are enchanted
            by the ghosts
            of an old farm house in North Dakota.
experiences which are curative
against blemished ambitions
            and gently ignored
            by our young ignorance
            of appreciating, but not really knowing
what we ourselves
have never encountered.

their stories are fractures
in our ribs
as we slowly breathe out
the subsistence of our departed
            sangre de sangre
            who come out
rolling the punches
and remembering the *relámpagos*
of their earthly existence,

slowly invading
space only the living
are given credit for.

      que en paz descansen

pero

      in another *cuento*,
we resurrect them
from a tomb of hidden memories

      that are passed on and on and on

      because without them

      our heirloom, our family

      vanishes
into a steady stream of wondering.

Yo Soy
by Lady Mariposa

Soy la muchachita morenita
with fingers woven into the chain link
fence outside of the community pool
that my *tía* hadn't paid her dues for.

Soy food stamp baby until 18,
ropa de la pulga,
& *abuela's cariños.*

Soy kissed by the sun,
black hair and dark eyes.
Soy returning home after *los trabajos*
ashamed of my *india* hues.

Soy looking into the mirror at 16
trying to believe myself beautiful.

Soy the shame of knowing that
I let them rip out my tongue.

Soy Chola en la academia.
Soy Chicana nacida from *semillas de libros.*

Soy la arbolita still trying to be an *árbol.*

AUTHOR BIOGRAPHIES

DIANE GONZALES BERTRAND was born and raised in the Woodlawn Lake area of San Antonio, Texas. Since 1992, she has been writing books for families to enjoy from romantic fiction set in San Antonio to award-winning bilingual picture books. Her novels include *Sweet Fifteen, Trino's Choice, Trino's Time,* and *The F Factor*. She is Writer-in-Residence at St. Mary's University where she teaches composition and creative writing. She is working on a collection of her poetry and another of short fiction for teens.

DAVID BOWLES resides in the Río Grande Valley of South Texas with his wife and children. Bowles launched his sci-fi series *D'Angelo Chronicles* in 2009. In April of 2011, Absey & Co. published *The Seed: Stories from the River's Edge,* a collection of his YA short stories. In 2012, Bowles teamed up with painter Noé Vela to create *Mexican Bestiary,* a bilingual encyclopedia of legendary Mexican creatures that has been nominated for the Tejas Star Book Award. Later this year, Lamar University Press will release *Flower, Song, Dance: Aztec and Mayan Poetry,* a collection of Mesoamerican verse translated by Bowles. He has served as editor for the *Along the River* anthology series, *Donna Hooks Fletcher: Life and Writings,* the magazine *Flashquake,* and *La Noria Literary Journal*. His book review column TOP SHELF appears each Thursday in *The Monitor,* a regional newspaper.

RUBÉN DEGOLLADO lives in Pharr, Texas with his wife Julie and sons, Elijah and Miqueas. His work has appeared in *Bilingual Review/Revista Bilingüe, Beloit Fiction Journal, Gulf Coast, Hayden's Ferry Review, Image, Relief,* and the anthologies *Texas Short Stories, Fantasmas,* and *Bearing the Mystery.* Recently he was a finalist in *American Short Fiction's* annual contest, *Glimmer Train's* Family Matters Contest, and *Bellingham Review's* 2010 Tobias Wolff Award. He was the Artist of the Month for *Image* in April of 2012. "A Map of Where I've Been" is an excerpt from the novel-in-progress, *Throw.*

CÉSAR DE LEÓN is a South Texas native and is pursuing his MFA in Creative Writing with a Certificate in Mexican American Studies at University of Texas—Pan American. Cesar's poetry is included in the anthology *Along the River 2: More Voices from the Rio Grande,* and University of Texas—Pan American's 2012 *Gallery* magazine. In 2012, Cesar received a Golden Circle Award from The University of Columbia Press for his poem "Us." Most recently Cesar's poetry appeared in the January 2013 Creative Writing issue of *The Monitor's Festiva* section.

XAVIER GARZA, born and raised in the Rio Grande Valley, is a prolific author, artist, and storyteller whose works focus primarily on his experiences growing up in the small border town of Rio Grande City in deep South Texas. He published his first book, *Creepy Creatures and other Cucuys,* in 2004 through Arte Público Press. *Lucha Libre: The Man in the Silver Mask* was released in 2005, and won an Honor Book,

Americas award, and received a starred review from *Críticas* Magazine. His other books include *Juan and the Chupacabras, Charro Claus and the Tejas Kid, Zulema and the Witch Owl,* and *Kid Cyclone Fights the Devil and Other Stories.* His seventh book, *Maximilian and the Mystery of the Guardian Angel,* was chosen by the American Library Association as a 2012 Pura Belpré Author Book Honor. A sequel to the book, *Maximilian and the Bingo Rematch,* is slated for release by Cinco Puntos Press in the summer of 2013.

ERIKA GARZA-JOHNSON grew up in Elsa, a city featured in this anthology's cover art. Garza-Johnson received her M.F.A. in Creative Writing from the University of Texas Pan American. She works at STC as an instructor of writing and lives in McAllen with her husband and her two beautiful children. She has been reading and performing her poetry in the Río Grande Valley since 2001. She is also the poetry editor for *New Border,* an anthology of Border literature to be published by the Texas A&M University Press. Her poetry has been featured online in La Bloga, Con Tinta, and Poets Against SB 1070. Her work has also appeared in *Texas Observer* and *Border Senses.*

KATHERINE HOERTH is the author of three poetry books: a collection titled *The Garden, Uprooted* and two chapbooks, *Among the Mariposas* and *The Garden of Dresses.* Her work has been published in journals including *Rattle, Boxcar,* and *Front Porch,* and she has been twice nominated for a Pushcart Prize. Katherine serves as Assistant Poetry

Editor of *Fifth Wednesday Journal* and teaches writing at University of Texas—Pan American. She lives in Edinburg, Texas, with her love, Bruno, and their many cats.

Myra Infante grew up in McAllen, Texas, a city in South Texas near the Mexican border. Between attending her father's small Pentecostal church, working with her family in the fields, and visiting Mexico every weekend, Myra amassed a colorful array of experiences that inspired her YA collection, *Combustible Sinners and Other Stories*. A teacher of high school English, she is currently working on her first novel.

Lady Mariposa was a *chola*. Then she went to college. Now she is an educated *chola*. She has an M.F.A. in Creative Writing from University of Texas—Pan American, and is currently working on her Ph.D. at Washington State University. Verónica Sandoval, as Lady Mariposa is also known, grew up in Sullivan City, Texas, the oldest daughter and a preacher's kid. Her spoken word album, *Hecha en El Valle: Spoken Word and Borderland Beats,* can be found on iTunes.

Guadalupe García McCall was born in Mexico and moved to Texas as a young girl, keeping close ties with family on both sides of the border. Trained in Theater Arts and English, she now teaches English/Language Arts at a junior high school. Her poems for adults have appeared in more than twenty literary journals. *Under the Mesquite*, her first book, was widely heralded, winning the 2013 Lee Bennett

Hopkins Poetry Award and the Pura Belpré Author Award, among many others. Her novel *Summer of the Mariposas* has met with similar acclaim and has been nominated for the Andre Norton Award for Young Adult Science Fiction and Fantasy. García McCall lives with her husband and their three sons in the San Antonio, Texas, area.

DANIEL GARCÍA ORDAZ, a.k.a. The Poet Mariachi, teaches English at McAllen Memorial High School and is the author of *You Know What I'm Sayin'?* from El Zarape Press. He is a former journalist and is also a founder of the Rio Grande Valley International Poetry Festival. He has been called "the voice of the Rio Grande Valley" by *The Monitor*'s book critic. Daniel was one of five writers and the only poet selected to participate in the Texas Latino Voices project in 2009.

AMALIA ORTIZ is a *tejana* performance poet and playwright who has appeared on three seasons of *Russell Simmons Presents Def Poetry* on HBO and the NAACP Image Awards on FOX. She has toured colleges and universities as a solo artist and with the performance-poetry troupes Diva Diction, the Chicano Messengers of Spoken Word, and the Def Poetry College Tour. She was awarded a writing residency at the National Hispanic Cultural Center. She is a CantoMundo Fellow and a Hedgebrook writer-in-residence alumna, where she wrote a Latino musical, *Carmen de la Calle*.

OCTAVIO QUINTANILLA is from the Río Grande Valley of South Texas. His poetry has appeared in *Alaska Quarterly Review, Los Angeles Review*, and elsewhere. His critical reviews have appeared in *Texas Books in Review* and in *Southwestern American Literature*. He teaches English at Texas A & M University—Kingsville.

DAVID RICE published his first collection of short fiction, *Give the Pig a Chance and Other Stories,* in 1996, and followed it up with two other highly regarded collections for young adult readers, *Crazy Loco: Stories* and *Heart Shaped Cookies and Other Stories*. He is a committed educator whose primary focus is to take part in creating a society that is educated, safe for families within a healthy environment, and dedicated to helping youth realize their potential to seek higher education opportunities. He has written and produced several movies that take place in deep South Texas where they are also filmed. He divides his time between Austin and South Texas. His next book, due out in 2013 from Dial Books for Young Readers, is called *My True Father*.

BRENDA NETTLES RIOJAS is the editor and host of *Corazón Bilingüe,* a weekly radio program and on-line journal. Her poetry has been published in a number of publications including *di-verse-city, Ribbons, 2008 Texas Poetry Calendar, Interstice* and *Ezra—An Online Journal of Translation*. Brenda has also written a book, *La Primera Voz Que Oi*, about her roots, her feelings on maternity, her love for her mother, and thoughts on religion.

José Antonio Rodríguez is the author of the poetry collection *The Shallow End of Sleep* (winner of the Bob Bush Memorial Award from the Texas Institute of Letters) and *Backlit Hour*. A former editor of the national literary journal *Harpur Palate*, he has also received the Allen Ginsberg Poetry Award and has been nominated three times for the Pushcart Prize. Rodríguez holds a Ph.D. in English and Creative Writing from State University of New York in Binghamton. Learn more at his website, www.JoseOrBust.blogspot.com.

René Saldaña, Jr., is the author of several books for young adults and children, among them *The Jumping Tree*, *Finding Our Way: Stories*, *The Whole Sky Full of Stars*, *A Good Long Way*, and *Dancing with the Devil and Other Tales from Beyond/Bailando Con El Diablo y Otros Cuentos del Mas Alla*. The third in his Mickey Rangel mystery series is due out in late 2013, and his first picture book, a bilingual counting book will be published in 2014. It's called *Dale, dale, dale: Una fiesta de números/Hit It, Hit It, Hit It: A Fiesta of Numbers*. He lives with his wife, Tina, and their children in Lubbock, Texas, where he is an associate professor in the College of Education at Texas Tech University.

Jan Seale, the 2012-13 Texas Poet Laureate, is a native Texan who lives in McAllen, in the southern tip of Texas. She is the author of seven volumes of poetry, two books of short fiction, three books of nonfiction, and nine children's books. Her writing has appeared in many magazines and newspapers including *The Yale Review, Texas Monthly, The Chicago Tribune,* and *Writer's Digest*. Some anthologies including her work are *Writing on the Wind, Let's Hear It!, Red Boots and Attitude, If I Had My Life to Live Over, Cries of the Spirit, Mixed Voices, This Place in Memory,* and *Birds in the Hand.*

PRISCILLA CELINA SUÁREZ is a *tejana* from the Rio Grande Valley whose poetry is a hybrid of *rancheras, polkas,* pop, R&B, rock, and yes, *música internacional.* She is a past recipient of the Mexicasa Writing Fellowship and is a current contributor to the American Library Association's *YALS* Magazine.

MINERVA VÁSQUEZ is a mother, teacher, and writer whose work has been featured in the *Along the River* anthology series and other venues. A home-grown resident of the Valley, she writes about events that have impacted her deeply.

EDWARD VIDAURRE, born in East L.A., has been featured in the June 7, 2011, La Bloga "On-Line Floricanto" issue, the Valley International Poetry Festival anthology, *Boundless 2011, Writers of the Rio Grande,* and *Along the River 2.* He will be published in *The Beatest State in the Nation,* an anthology of Texas Beat poetry forthcoming by UT Press in 2013.

igs photos 2013